FiNCH

PENNY MATTHEWS

WALKER BOOKS
AND SUBSIDIARIES

LONDON • BOSTON • SYDNEY • AUCKLAND

First published in 2018
by Walker Books Australia Pty Ltd
Locked Bag 22, Newtown
NSW 2042 Australia
www.walkerbooks.com.au

Text © 2018 Penny Matthews

National Library of Australia Cataloguing-in-Publication entry:
Matthews, Penny, author.
Finch / Penny Matthews.
ISBN: 978 1 760650 75 9 (paperback)
For children.
Subjects: Modern & contemporary fiction

COVER IMAGE: Pexels.com/@luizclas-170497;
INTERNAL IMAGE: barka/Shutterstock

Cover Design: Mubu Design
Typeset in Adobe Caslon Pro
Printed and bound in Australia by Griffin Press

FSC
www.fsc.org
MIX
Paper from
responsible sources
FSC® C009448

The paper this book is printed on is certified against the
Forest Stewardship Council® Standards. Griffin Press holds
FSC chain of custody certification SGS-COC-005088. FSC
promotes environmentally responsible, socially beneficial
and economically viable management of the world's forests.

For Viv

CHAPTER 1

Audrey lay in bed, ears alert, listening. It was her first night in the old farmhouse, and she couldn't sleep. It was so hot! And her bedroom smelled funny, sort of mouldy.

She heard a creak. *What was that?*

Mouse-like squeaking and scratching as a gust of wind pushed tree branches against her bedroom window.

Then silence.

Deep, deep silence.

No traffic. No friendly streetlights to lighten the dark square of the window blind. Being in the country was definitely not like being in the city.

I wish I was home again. I wish, I wish, I wish …

And then she heard something else. At first it sounded like someone moaning. Then came a rising wail, a sound so eerie, so piercingly sad, that she felt the hair rise on the back of her neck.

It's a ghost!

Of course it's not. There's no such thing.

Who says? This place is old, it's creepy–

Listen to it! It's a dog howling. It's just a dog.

The sound came again, heartbreaking in its misery. Audrey pulled her pillow over her head, but she couldn't block it out. It seemed to reach right into her brain.

The dog stopped howling at last. But then a new sound started up, *inside* the house.

It was Freddy, wanting to be let out.

Audrey climbed out of bed and made her way down the dark hallway, stubbing her toe on a large packing crate outside the kitchen door. *Ouch! Stupid box!*

Freddy was on the window ledge in the sitting room. As soon as he heard Audrey he turned around, tail up, and made a hopeful noise, half-meow, half-purr.

"Sorry, Fred, I can't let you out," Audrey whispered. She carried Freddy back to her bedroom, closed the door and switched on the bedside lamp. The big white-and-tabby cat wandered around the strange room for a while and then stretched up high on his back legs to look out the window, pushing the blind aside with his head. Finally he jumped up on the bed, snuggled into the curve of Audrey's body and began to purr loudly.

Audrey turned off the light.

The morning was hot and sunny, completely ghost-free. Ten-year-old Chloe, Audrey's younger sister, was exploring the big backyard. "Look, I found some chook eggs under the tank-stand! I bet they're about a thousand years old." "There are ducks on the dam! Quick, come and see!" "Audrey, Audrey, I found a horseshoe! That's for good luck, isn't it?"

Obviously Chloe wasn't too fussed about living here. Nothing much bothered Chlo for long.

When they'd arrived late yesterday afternoon they'd made the beds so that everyone had somewhere to sleep. Most of the packing crates still had to be sorted out, though. Two of them were labelled "Audrey's things", neatly printed in black texta, and one had "Chloe's stuff PRIVATE" written on it inside a big scrawled pink love heart. The removal men had already put nearly all the furniture in the right rooms, but a few bits and pieces still stood around like awkward guests, getting in the way.

After breakfast they started to get everything organised. They put books in bookcases, and worked out where to hang pictures and what to do with odd chairs. Audrey stuck her bird poster on her bedroom wall with Blu-Tack and arranged her owl collection on the windowsill. Freddy prowled around, sniffing all the unfamiliar smells, and had his tail trodden on twice.

The rooms in the farmhouse were quite small, and their living-room furniture looked all wrong. It was too large, too modern, too … too *city*.

"They didn't waste money on big rooms, those early settlers," said Dad. "Good for the environment, too. Easier to heat, and those solid walls keep the place cool in summer."

Mum didn't reply. She just went on wiping

things down with a duster, straightening up every so often to ease her back. Audrey knew Mum didn't want to live in the country. It had been totally Dad's idea. Dad had worked for a manufacturing firm, but he'd been laid off – *made redundant* – more than a year ago. He'd looked for another job for months. And then, without warning, he'd decided that they should all move to the country. A tree change, he called it.

He'd found their new home advertised in the local newspaper. "Live your dream!" the ad had said. "The perfect hobby farm! Character farmhouse on 30 hectares of prime country, just minutes from the beach. Five hectares of vines already planted to shiraz and cabernet sauvignon."

Dad loved the idea of owning a vineyard, and the property was quite close to a town with the usual shops and services, and most importantly a big area school that taught up to Year Twelve. The main problem was that there weren't any jobs for Mum. She'd worked for years as a legal secretary. She loved her job, and for the whole time Dad had been out of work she'd kept the family going. Now all she could be was a farmer's wife. (A *vigneron's* wife, Dad had told her, as if that was somehow better.) Right from the beginning she'd told Dad she didn't want to be a farmer's wife, or even a vigneron's wife, but Dad had talked her into it. "Wait till we're settled, Caroline," he'd said. "Give it a chance, at least."

By midday the house was more or less in order, and Mum called everyone into the kitchen for lunch. The pots and frying pans and plates and mugs and knives and spoons and forks had all found their places in the kitchen cupboards and drawers, and the toaster and the electric kettle had done their best to make the counter look familiar.

Mum got a quiche out of the fridge and sliced up a loaf of crusty bread that had gone soft and leathery. She buttered the bread and Audrey poured juice for herself and Chloe while Dad made coffee in the plunger. Mum gave Dad a tight little smile when he handed her a mug of coffee.

After lunch, Dad took them all on a guided tour. "There are fences that divide our land from the land that belongs to our neighbours," he said. "I needn't tell you girls that you stay within those boundaries. You don't just wander on to someone else's property. That's called trespassing, and it's something country people take very seriously, okay? It's like walking into somebody else's home when you haven't been invited."

Their farm was on low hilly country and surrounded by other low hills patched with other vineyards. Far to the west you could see the sea, a faint blue line ruled between land and sky. A breeze softened the heat of the sun. It was summer, still the school holidays.

Audrey followed her parents up the hill, feeling the dry grass brush against her bare legs. To her left was the vineyard that had been the reason Dad had bought the farm. Rows of vines loaded with bunches of dark grapes stretched towards the northern boundary fence. As the family approached, there was an explosion of wings, and a flock of starlings rose into the air.

"We'll have to do something about *that*," said Dad. "Damn pests, getting fat on my crop."

The starlings flew off, shrieking, and Dad stopped to pick a bunch of grapes. He tasted a couple of berries, spat them out, and offered the bunch to Mum. "Have a taste. They're not ready yet – not enough sugar. They'll need another month or so."

Mum took a berry, but didn't put it in her mouth.

She was gazing towards the western horizon. "Quite a good view from here," she said.

Dad looked relieved. "It's a pretty place, Caroline. And I'll make it work. Trust me."

Trust Dad? Look where that got us, Audrey thought. He'd turned their lives topsy-turvy. Like Mum, Audrey had hated leaving the city. Life in the suburbs was all she'd ever known. And the idea of having to get used to a new school, a *country* school, panicked her a bit. Would a country school be different from a city one? Would the kids be different? She'd looked forward to being a senior at St Cuthbert's and having her name listed on the back of her year's jumper. Now all that had gone, along with the school where she had, if not real friends, then at least sort-of friends.

She thought about those sort-of friends now, and wondered if she'd miss them. Maybe, a little. Would they miss her? Probably not. Some of them might keep in touch for a while; Jaz would, at least. Jasmine Chen was everyone's friend, which meant she was Audrey's friend too, and the nearest Audrey had to a proper friend. She was smart and pretty, and on the A netball team. Jaz always put lots of stuff on

Instagram – selfies taken on holidays, clothes she'd just bought, photos of her cute Cavoodle puppy.

Audrey never posted anything online about herself – partly because she didn't have a mobile phone, and partly because she didn't think her life was interesting enough. Jaz was always teasing her about it. "Omigod, Aud, you are *so* boring," she'd told her, once. She'd laughed when she said it, though, so Audrey would know she didn't really mean it.

I'll go on my laptop tonight and see what everyone's doing, Audrey decided. It was so annoying that Dad wouldn't let her have a mobile phone. "Can't afford it," he'd said. "Ask me again when you're in Year Eight. Or Year Nine. Or even better, Year Twelve." He started to mutter about wasting money, and too much screen time, and kids not knowing how dangerous social media could be. "I know all that, Dad, and I'd be super careful," Audrey had said, but of course he didn't listen.

No wonder I always feel like I'm different, she thought. All *the kids I know have their own phone. Every single one of them. Jaz had her first iPhone when she was* eight.

While Mum and Dad wandered down the rows

of vines, Audrey and Chloe went up the hill towards the furthest boundary fence. The breeze was stronger here. Chloe's long ponytail streamed out behind her, and Audrey's short, silky hair lifted around her head, cooling her scalp.

From the top of the hill they could see the farmhouse and its outbuildings, doll-sized in the distance, the half-empty dam with its water-level rings, and the old orchard. Further away, a creek wound off into the distance.

"Our farm is big, isn't it?" Chloe said brightly, pulling strands of windblown hair away from her face. "Bigger than I thought, anyway."

"I guess."

"I think it'll be fun living here, don't you?"

"Seriously? No."

Chloe's face fell, and Audrey felt a twinge of guilt. After all, none of this was Chloe's fault. She put an arm around her. "I mean," she said, "I don't know. Whether it's going to be fun, that is."

Chloe looked happy again. "We can *make* it fun."

"Sure." Audrey forced a smile.

As they stood looking out over their new home, they heard a faint meow. Freddy was trotting through the grass towards them, bounding over the high tussocks. He made a beeline for Audrey and rubbed affectionately against her legs.

"Hi, Fred! Did you miss us?" Audrey picked him up and draped him around her neck, a purring fur collar. Freddy was so friendly, so easily pleased, so uncomplicated. He always made her feel better.

But going on Instagram that evening, sitting up in bed, made her feel worse again. Everyone she knew was going to parties or sleepovers, or they were staying at their family's beach house, or they'd gone interstate or overseas for their holidays. *Bali is amazing,* Jaz posted, along with a photo of herself in a pair of trendy metallic sunglasses with pink lenses. She was smiling and doing a thumbs up.

Audrey looked at the image for a while and then closed down her laptop.

CHAPTER 2

When Audrey was very little, her grandma had shown her a big book with illustrations of all kinds of birds – jewel-coloured hummingbirds, bright pink flamingos with long and unbelievably skinny legs, tiny blue wrens, flame-chested robins. It soon became Audrey's favourite book, and every time she visited her grandma she asked to see it again.

By the time she was six or seven she could identify all the birds she saw in their garden at home, and in the local park. When she wasn't much older, she'd started to learn their almost impossible-to-pronounce scientific names, reading them aloud from a field guide. "*Phylidonyris novaehollandiae*," she would say slowly, putting her finger under each syllable. "*Rhipidura leucophrys*." Anyone could identify a New Holland honeyeater or a willie wagtail by their common names, but knowing their proper names made you feel as if you were a member of a special club. If you used those names, people from all over the world would know exactly which bird you were talking about.

Audrey had never been very interested in the things most girls liked when they were in junior primary – Barbie dolls and fairy princesses and ballet and make-up and doing each other's hair. She thought of these as "pink things". She could see why other girls enjoyed them, but they weren't for her. Instead, birds became her passion.

For her ninth birthday, her grandpa had built her a big wooden-framed birdcage. Mum and Dad gave her three pairs of zebra finches, and the whole family enjoyed watching them flitting between the nest boxes and splashing in the water bowl. They were small and quick and neat, with brilliant red beaks and striped or spotted feathers, white and brown and grey. Audrey loved the way they burst into a chorus of squeaky chattering whenever they were alarmed, which was about every five minutes.

The pairs began to breed. Small round white eggs appeared in the nests, and soon newly hatched chicks, adorable bundles of grey fluff, were hopping around on the floor of the cage. Before long the six birds had become twelve. To keep the cage from becoming overcrowded Audrey raided the nests every few days, gathering up handfuls of eggs and throwing them away. Within a couple of years the older birds began to die off, the females going first.

Now the cage stood on its four sturdy legs next to the glory vine on the back verandah of the farmhouse. It was home to five elderly male birds. Mum had suggested naming them after the five Marx Brothers, film star comedians from the 1930s. Groucho, Harpo, Chico, Zeppo and Gummo spent their lives maintaining the pecking order. Groucho, a fine plump bird with chestnut cheek patches, was in charge, and then came his four brothers, the state of their feathers showing their ranking. At the bottom of the pecking order was Gummo, a small buff-coloured bird with no neck feathers at all.

Audrey was fond of all her birds, but especially

Gummo. She knew what it was like to be at the bottom of the pecking order – you had to keep your head down. She'd decided long ago that it was best not to tell the girls at school about her fascination with birds, or that one day she planned to study them properly. She was sure they'd think she was weird; probably they'd laugh about her behind her back. Even Jaz thought that Audrey only liked clothes and shopping, stuff like that. And *boys*. Audrey thought most of the boys in her class were annoying, but the other girls giggled and gossiped about them all the time, so she pretended to be interested too. She knew that Jaz would put birds in the worst category of all: *Bor-ing*. Privately, Audrey thought Jaz could be a bit boring herself sometimes, but it was hard not to like her. She was fun to be around. And it was useful having a friend, even a sort-of friend, who was popular. It helped her to fit in.

Audrey had never had a proper best friend, someone she could really talk to. Chloe, on the other hand, collected best friends the way Audrey collected owl ornaments. One week she'd talk only about Candice or Shakira; the next week it would be Sienna or Madison or Ruby. Sometimes the old best friend was upset and became an enemy for a short time, but mostly all that happened was that the circle of friends just grew a little larger.

If Chloe was a bird, Audrey thought, *she'd be a rainbow lorikeet: bright, inquisitive, a bit loud, often part of a large flock*. She herself would be a tawny frogmouth: shy and solitary, good at not being noticed. She managed to seem average in most ways. Not bad at lessons, not bad at sport, no trouble in class. Not pretty, but not ugly either. Nothing special about her at all.

On the afternoon of their second day on the farm Dad drove them all into town. "We can have a look around and then go for a coffee," he said. "I saw a little place in the main street that looked quite promising." Audrey hadn't taken much notice of the town whenever they'd driven through it earlier, before it had so quickly and unexpectedly become a part of their lives. Now she looked at it differently.

Dad slowed down as they drove past the school, a large red-brick building on the outskirts of town.

It looked neat and well cared for, cleaned up and refreshed over the long summer holidays, ready to spring into action. A line of yellow school buses waited on one side of the car park for the new term to start. In the distance somebody was pushing a wheelbarrow; magpies strolled around on the lush green lawn, listening for worms and nimbly avoiding the long arcs of water spraying from the sprinklers. *Gymnorhina tibicen*, Audrey thought, her mind automatically going into bird-identification mode. She loved magpies – they were amazingly intelligent, and their singing was the happiest, best sound ever. But why did they have so many different songs? What did the songs mean? It was like magpies talked to each other, *really* talked–

"There's your palace of learning, kids," Dad said. "Impressive, I'd say, for a country school. Nice grounds, plenty of trees."

"It's heaps bigger than our old school," Chloe said. "I wonder where our classrooms are, Aud?"

"Who knows?" said Audrey, looking vaguely at the long rows of gleaming windows. She was still thinking about magpies, and she didn't particularly care where her classroom was. All she hoped for was that school wouldn't be the dreary, lonely experience she was sure it would be. Even the school uniform was dreary. Brown! Why couldn't it be blue, or dark green, like the St Cuthbert's uniform? *Brown is such a nothing colour,* Audrey thought. *I've already got brown hair, brown eyes. I guess the uniform could be a sort of camouflage – I could just disappear into it, like a frogmouth. Or a boobook owl. Ninox novaeseelandiae.*

Dad drove slowly for a short distance, and then pulled into a parking spot. "Let's take a walk down the main drag."

Dutifully, Audrey got out of the car. There weren't many people around, and the street seemed depressingly empty. They wandered past a hardware store with bales of pea straw and bags of fertiliser piled up outside the front door, and a place that sold tractors and ride-on mowers and various unfamiliar pieces of agricultural machinery, all brand-new and lollipop-shiny with bright red and yellow and green paint. Further down the street they came to what Audrey supposed was the centre of town, with a post office, a bakery, a real estate business with faded, curling photographs of rural properties tacked up on a board, a fairly big supermarket, a

Chinese restaurant and a gift shop that sold pottery and hand-painted scarves and dreamcatchers. The gift shop was closed, and there were several dead blowflies in the window.

"Here's the place," Dad said, stopping outside a small cafe. "Goosey Gander. Silly name."

"I rather like it," said Mum. It was the first time she'd spoken since they'd left the farm. "It's fun and quirky."

"Well, I'm glad you approve, Caroline," Dad said in a falsely hearty voice. "Let's go in. Kids, you can have something to eat if you want. A treat."

Inside, the walls of the cafe were hung with prints of white geese wandering through flowery fields or in English farmyards with stables and haystacks. A papier-mâché goose in a bonnet and a frilly apron sat on a swing suspended over the counter.

"*So* cute," said Chloe. She looked up at the menu, which was written on a blackboard. "Can I have a strawberry milkshake?" she asked the woman behind the counter. "And a ... a ... a piece of chocolate mud cake. With lots of cream."

"Whatever you want, Princess," said Dad, still falsely hearty. "What about you, Audrey? Caroline?"

"A latte for me," Mum said.

"Vanilla milkshake, please," said Audrey. She knew that was boring, but she couldn't think of anything else. "And maybe a Florentine."

"So that's our town," Dad said, as they sat down at a small, rather rickety table. "All your needs catered for. Not so bad, is it?"

"I suppose not," said Mum. "Or to put it another way, it could be worse."

Audrey stared at the china sugar bowl, on which were still more geese, this time with blue ribbons tied in bows around their necks. Of course the town wasn't bad. It was probably quite a nice town, as country towns went. Still, it was unfamiliar. Unknown. Different.

Right now all she wanted was to go home.

CHAPTER 3

They'd been on the farm for just four days when they met Mavis. She came to the back door early in the morning carrying a basket of cucumbers, the prickly pale green kind nobody liked, with big tough seeds.

"Thought I should pay a visit to my new next-door neighbours," she said. "I live just down the road, the house with cactuses in the front. I reckoned you could use some cucumbers. They're real nice with a bit of vinegar dressing."

Mavis was tall and thin, with tanned, leathery skin and bright blue eyes. She was wearing a red John Deere baseball cap, a faded tartan shirt and a pair of old corduroy trousers. She didn't wait to be invited in, but walked straight into the kitchen, put her basket on the table and sat down. "Don't mind me," she said in a raspy, smoky voice. "I know this house like the back of my hand. The people you bought it from were relations of mine."

"Oh, you mean the Kepplers?" said Mum, hovering behind her chair. "Can I get you a cup of tea, Mrs–?"

"Mavis," said their visitor. She took off her cap, revealing white hair that stuck up like a brush. "Thanks, I'd love one. Yeah, Jack Keppler married my sister. He ended up with cancer – we reckon he got it from all the weedkiller he used. Now he's dead and she's in a nursing home. Their son Trevor ran this place."

Mum switched on the electric jug and put tea bags in mugs. "I'm Caroline, and these two are Audrey and Chloe. (Audrey, can you get the biscuits out for me, please?) Ian's gone in to town to see about some irrigation equipment."

"No worries, I'll meet him another time. No one's a stranger around here. You need to look out for each other in the country. My brother lives over the way. He's on his own, so I check up on him most days. He's not been too well lately. Reckon the poor old bloke might be on the way out."

"Oh, I'm sorry to hear that," said Mum politely. "Is he very old?"

"Older than me. We all have to go when it's our time, don't we?" She peered into the biscuit container and picked out a custard cream. "Ta. I'll wait till I have my cuppa, so I can soften this up a bit." She grinned, and Audrey saw with horror that she didn't have any teeth.

Audrey raised her eyebrows at Mum, indicating the door, and Mum nodded. She grabbed Chloe by the arm and the two of them, smothering laughter, made their escape. They ran down to the far end of the yard and collapsed on the patch of clover lawn under the rotary clothes line.

"Chlo, did you see? She's got no teeth!"

"I know! And her fingers are all yellow." Chloe shuddered. "*So* gross. She must've smoked her entire life."

"Dad says country people smoke more than city people."

"Do they? Why?"

"Who knows?" Audrey said. "We don't know any country people."

"We will soon. School in a week, yay!"

Audrey made a face. "Did you have to remind me? I bet all they talk about is cows and tractors."

"And that's just the girls!"

Audrey's laugh turned into a sigh. "I wish we didn't have to leave St Cuthbert's. I was happy there."

"No, you weren't, Aud. You didn't like St Cuthbert's either."

This was too close to the truth. To be honest, Audrey didn't really fit in anywhere. She knew it, but it was kind of humiliating that Chloe knew it too.

She stared through the wires of the clothes line up at the sky. When she half-closed her eyes against the sunlight, all she could see were dazzling golden sparkles. She tried to imagine that she was in a different world, a place where everything was shining and beautiful, filled with undiscovered treasures, spangled with gold. The sort of magical place she used to dream about when she was small. No scary new school, no quarrelling parents, no weird old ladies without any teeth … She let her mind drift.

"Hey, Aud?"

"Yes?"

"D'you think that old lady was trespassing? She walked into our house when she wasn't invited, didn't she?"

Audrey sat up. "You're right, Chlo. Like Dad says, we should take that *very seriously.*"

They both lay back on the lawn, giggling.

Mavis chatted to Mum for nearly an hour, so by the time she left Mum had a headache and was in a really bad mood. Dad came home for lunch in a bad mood too: the irrigation parts he needed for the vineyard weren't available from the hardware store and had to be ordered in. They had cold meat without tomato sauce for lunch, and one of Mavis's cucumbers. It was almost inedible, all big yellow seeds and bitter flesh.

Halfway through lunch, Mum and Dad began to argue. Again.

Without a word, Audrey and Chloe pushed back their chairs, stood up and left the table. They went outside and looked at each other.

"Creek?" asked Audrey.

Chloe nodded.

They ran through the backyard and then raced down the slope that led to the creek, each trying to beat the other. Audrey won. Running was one of the things she could still do better than Chloe.

They stood on the bank of the creek, panting.

Audrey looked to the left, and then to the right. "Shall we see where it goes?"

"Okay."

"Watch out for snakes. You have to stamp your feet hard so you scare them away."

They turned right and stamped along the bank, even though there wasn't nearly enough grass for snakes to hide in. Soon they stopped stamping and just walked. The creek bed was almost dry. Occasionally, in between stretches of rock and sand, there were shallow pools of brownish water.

Audrey stopped every so often to peer into a pool or turn over a stone. "Look, Chlo, a skink!" she said, delighted. She crouched, watching as a tiny shining lizard scuttled away in a panic to hide under a rock. "And there's lots of things in the water, too – there's wrigglers and backswimmers and water boatmen—"

Chloe sighed loudly. "In other words, yucky bugs."

"They're not yucky – they're interesting. Once you start looking, there's heaps to see. Except wrigglers means mosquitoes, ugh. I can't see any tadpoles, but they could be here soon. How brilliant would it be to have tadpoles! We could have a frog colony! I wonder what sort of frogs they'd be?"

"Boring." Chloe gave an exaggerated yawn. "Who cares about frogs?"

Audrey stood up. "Chlo, why do you always have to say things like that? It's not like you even believe it. I don't know why I put up with you."

"Because you're a nerdy Nerd Girl, and I'm your only friend."

Audrey knew Chloe didn't really mean it: it was just something she said, like Jaz did. *Only joking.* Still, it hurt. She opened her mouth to reply, and then closed it again. It was better to say nothing, because she knew Chlo hated to be ignored.

"Sorry, Aud," Chloe said after a while. "Love you."

"I know," said Audrey. "Love you too. Mostly."

They walked on in companionable silence, sisters again.

"What's that?" Audrey pointed to a piece of metal sticking out of gravelly sand in a dry part of the creek bed. They dug with their hands and pulled it out. It was the remains of an iron frying pan, and there was more buried rubbish close by: a tangle of rusted wire, a badly worn enamel plate, something that had once been a kettle.

Audrey held the frying pan between her finger and thumb, then dropped it and kicked sand over it. "I wonder who it belonged to."

"Someone who didn't know you shouldn't litter," Chloe said, looking virtuous.

After a while they reached the boundary of their farm, a chicken-wire fence topped with a double strand of barbed wire. The creek continued, winding through a tumble of rocks, but now it ran through somebody else's property.

The air was very still – not the smallest breath of wind. Audrey felt that the countryside all around her was expectant, waiting for something. But waiting for what?

Beneath a bright sky the rocks seemed to

shimmer. Flying high, a lone sulphur-crested cockatoo shone white against the blue. Its harsh cry tore at the silence.

Audrey tilted her head to follow its flight. "*Cacatua galerita*," she said.

"*Caca*," said Chloe, at her elbow. "You sound so ... so *prentious*."

"You mean *pretentious*," Audrey corrected her. Something else had caught her eye. "See that crooked gum tree? Way further down, where the rocks are really steep? Look at that dark shadow underneath it. D'you think it's a cave?"

"Maybe." Chloe strained to see. "It's too far away. Want to go and have a look?"

Audrey stared at the distant shadow. It both attracted and repelled her in a way she couldn't explain. There was something strange, something ... *otherworldly* about it. But that was silly, wasn't it? A cave – if it was a cave – was just a hollow in the rocks. A geological formation. She gave herself a mental shake. "We shouldn't. It's not on our land. You know what Dad said."

"Nobody'll see us, Aud. Come on, you wanted to explore. It'll be fun."

"I don't feel like it. Really. We ought to go home."

Chloe sagged. "Whatever."

Audrey started to make her way back along the creek. "Let's see if Mum and Dad have killed each other yet." She tried to sound casual.

That evening they spent hours trying to get their TV to work. There was no aerial on the roof because, according to Mavis, Trevor Keppler had taken it away to use on his beach shack. The old rabbit ears Mum had found didn't work. They'd have to get a proper aerial. A proper smart TV would be good, too, but there wasn't much chance of that.

Audrey could see that Dad was getting more and more irritated by all the little things that were going wrong. So far, apart from the irrigation and the television, he'd had to cope with a leaky toilet, loose corrugated iron on the roof and the unpleasant discovery that the dam had been used as a rubbish tip. The water level was dropping, and the slimed-over remains of an old car and bits of farm machinery could be seen just below the surface.

"Those Kepplers must have been real bogans," said Dad. "God knows what's in there. Probably a few bodies."

"Gross," said Chloe. "We found lots of rubbish down the creek too, didn't we, Aud?"

"Well," said Mum, in a "told-you-so" sort of voice, "what did you expect?"

Audrey glanced at Dad, but he didn't seem to have heard.

After dinner, with the TV dark and silent in the corner of the living room, they sat around the kitchen table and played Monopoly.

"I don't like this game," said Chloe, after a while. She was hopelessly in debt and becoming grumpy. "I'm going to bed."

"You just want to quit because you've only got a house in Kent Town," Audrey told her. She had three houses on Park Lane, a hotel on Regent Street, two railway stations and both utilities, and she was feeling rather pleased with herself. Usually it was Chloe who managed to collect all the valuable properties.

"Game over," said Dad. "Audrey, you are officially declared the winner."

Mum collected the cards, sorted them out and put them in tidy piles. "Personally I'd be quite happy with a house in Kent Town," she said. "Or anywhere in a city, for that matter."

There was a short silence.

"Well," said Dad coldly. "I'm sorry you still feel like that, Caroline. Goodnight, girls. See you in the morning."

The pleasure Audrey had felt at winning Monopoly vanished. She hated it when Mum and Dad didn't get along, and they had been fighting, on and off, for ages. The possibility that they might separate terrified her. It had happened to lots of kids at St Cuthbert's. Jaz's mum and dad were divorced, and Jaz had to spend half her holidays with her mum in Adelaide and the other half in Sydney with her dad, who was a lawyer and very rich. She always came back from Sydney with new clothes, or a new game, or a bag of fun things from Smiggle. Once, her dad had given her a pair of brightly enamelled parrot earrings. Audrey would have given almost anything for earrings like that, but so far she hadn't even had her ears pierced. "Not until you're in Year Eight," Mum always said. Not too long to wait now, unless Mum had changed her mind. (Wow, in Year Eight she could maybe have pierced ears *and* a phone!)

Jaz said it wasn't too bad having parents in two different cities. She said you got used to it, and as a bonus they always gave you heaps of great stuff. Her dad had a new girlfriend who was really cool, like a big sister. But Audrey knew that, for her, nothing could make up for the worst situation she could imagine – herself and Chloe and Mum and Dad not all being together.

She got into bed and huddled under the quilt with a hollow feeling in her stomach.

CHAPTER 4

Audrey never forgot what happened that night.

Once again she couldn't sleep. She lay staring at the ceiling and trying not to think of all the things that could go wrong in the future: Mum and Dad ... this horrible farm ... the new school, probably horrible too ... not knowing anyone here (Mavis didn't count) ... pimples (she could feel one starting on her chin) ...

The glowing red figures on her alarm clock moved silently to 12.00. The roof creaked. Tree branches squeaked and scrabbled against the window.

Suddenly the night was ripped apart by a

bloodcurdling yowl. It was so intense and so loud that a white light flashed behind Audrey's eyes like a bolt of lightning. What was happening? *Freddy!*

She raced down the hall and switched on the sitting-room light. "Freddy?" she called. "Fred?"

A low growling sound came from the window. The curtains were closed, and between them hung a motionless tail, its fur so erect that it looked like a bottlebrush. When Audrey pulled back the curtains, Freddy didn't turn to greet her. He kept his head pressed to the window, staring out.

"What is it, Fred? It's okay. It's okay."

Her hands trembling, Audrey began to stroke Freddy's head and back, pressing down in what she hoped was a soothing way. Freddy continued to growl deep in his throat, a sound at once terrified and threatening.

Audrey gazed out the window. The moon was full, and the garden was a mass of spiky shadows.

One of the shadows seemed to be moving.

Freddy growled again, and then hissed, teeth bared.

It looked like another cat was in the garden – a big one. Probably a feral. Audrey had read about feral cats wandering around the country, pets dumped by people who no longer wanted them. She felt sorry for animals like that: imagine how they'd feel, trusting their owners, thinking they were loved, and then being thrown out like a piece of rubbish. The awful thing, the terrible thing, was that feral cats killed so many native creatures. Still–

The animal moved out of the shadows.

Audrey felt a jolt of surprise. Not a cat. A dog. A fox terrier, by the look of it. Quite small for a dog, hardly any bigger than Freddy.

She gave Freddy a gentle scratch between the ears. "You silly old cat. It's not anything to be afraid of. It's only a little dog."

Chloe's hot breath was in her ear.

"What was that noise? Was it Freddy?"

"Of course it was Freddy. He saw something in the garden and went off his head. I thought it was another cat, but it was a dog. I heard a dog howling the first night we were here – it must have been this one. Look."

She turned back to the window and pointed. But there was nothing there, just the garden, quiet in the moonlight.

At breakfast everything was all right again. Mum was frying bacon and eggs, and Dad was pouring orange juice. Bright sunlight streamed through the window.

"Did you hear Freddy last night?" asked Audrey.

"I certainly did," said Mum. She handed out plates of bacon and eggs, and then sat down at the table. "Pepper grinder, please, Chlo. I also heard you get up to investigate, Audrey. What was the problem?"

"I thought there must be another cat outside," said Audrey. "You know how Fred hates other cats. But it turned out it was a dog."

"A *dog*? In our garden? In the middle of the night?"

"Why not? Maybe it was lost."

"Dogs aren't nocturnal animals," said Dad. "They aren't like cats. Even if it *was* lost, I can't imagine it would be roaming around at that time. It'd be curled up asleep somewhere."

Audrey carefully cut the rind off her bacon.

"Well, this one wasn't asleep. It was a fox terrier, I think. I couldn't see it too well."

"I didn't see it at all," said Chloe, "but it sure got Freddy going. You should've seen his tail! It was like a hundred times its normal size!"

"Maybe the dog slipped its chain," said Dad. "Country people usually keep their dogs chained up. You don't want a pack of dogs mauling your sheep or eating your chooks."

"It could be Mavis's dog," Mum said, looking thoughtful. "She told me she's got a mutt that keeps her company. Audrey, I think you should check it out with her. Say her dog was on the loose last night and you saw it in our garden. She'll need to know."

"Do I have to? Why don't you or Dad go?"

"It's called being *neighbourly*, my girl. It's important to know who your neighbours are. And Mavis is perfectly pleasant. I know she's a bit chatty, but she's probably lonely." Mum put on her no-nonsense expression. "Anyway, I'm asking you to go and see her this morning. I don't have her phone number. You can take Chloe with you."

It was Chloe's turn to protest. "Mu-um!"

"Oh, for heaven's sake," said Dad. "Do what your

mother says, can't you? You can go straight after breakfast."

"We have to do the *dishes* straight after breakfast, Dad," Chloe grumbled. "Now that we don't have a *dishwasher* any more."

Dad glared at her. "That's enough, Chloe! No more arguments."

Mum gave Chloe a reproachful look and for the next few minutes there was silence, broken only by the sounds of toast crunching and a tap dripping.

After breakfast, Dad went out to check the vineyard, and Mum went to have her shower. Audrey and Chloe did the breakfast dishes, Chloe keeping up a sulky monologue: "I *hate* not having a dishwasher! Drying dishes is *such* a waste of time. Audrey, you're not washing properly. This fork has egg on it. It's all stuck between the prongs, yuck ..."

Audrey went on washing and stacking – Chloe always got things out of her system faster if you left her alone – and when she'd finished, and wiped down the sink and the counter, she went outside to feed her birds.

As usual, the moment she opened the hatch in their cage, they set up their usual agitated cheeping and fluttering. It was amazing, she thought, as she filled their bowl with millet seeds, that after so many years they'd never got used to her. They were aviary-bred, but wildness had been hard-wired into their tiny brains.

Audrey couldn't help feeling sorry for her finches. In a way it was her fault they had such dull lives. She'd read an article recently that said zebra finches used to live wild in these hills, great big flocks of them. Nobody ever saw them here now, although there were still thousands of them further inland. It was the same with budgerigars – in the outback they sometimes travelled in giant swarms, like bees, looking for food. There was a film about it she'd seen on YouTube. (Wild budgies were only ever green and yellow. Why was that?)

As she reached in for the water dish, she noticed that Gummo was having trouble flying. He hopped and fluttered, but although he tried to lift himself into the air he wasn't able to join his brothers on their perches.

"Hi, Gummo," said Audrey. "What's the matter with you?" She looked more closely. It seemed that one of the little bird's wings wasn't working properly.

Freddy walked up to the cage and slid around Audrey's legs, meowing and looking up at the birds. The finches flew into the air in a panic, all except for Gummo, who hopped helplessly around on the cage floor. Freddy's yellow eyes widened. He reached upwards, putting his front paws on the wire mesh.

"Go *away*, Fred," said Audrey. She gave the cat a light smack on the ear, and Freddy sank reluctantly to the ground. "Leave my birds alone!"

The back screen door creaked open, and Chloe came outside. She had changed into her favourite pink-striped sundress and fuchsia Crocs. "Let's go see that old lady now and get it over with," she said. "Mum'll go all weird on us otherwise."

Audrey sighed. "Why are we doing this, again?"

"We have to tell her about her *dog*." Chloe peered into the cage. "Those finches do a lot of poo," she said, wrinkling her nose. "There's poo in their drinking water, too."

"I know, the cage needs cleaning. We could do it together. It'd be much faster that way."

"You have got to be joking, Aud. Let's get going."

Audrey got going.

CHAPTER 5

Mavis's plain red-brick house looked like a giant Lego building. A picket fence surrounded a garden filled with different kinds of cactus. In the middle a plaster gnome sat on the edge of a birdbath, his fishing line dangling into the empty blue-painted bowl.

Chloe giggled. "Think he'll ever catch anything?"

"Not likely. Poor gnome, waiting his entire life for something that's never going to happen."

Apart from the gnome, there was a pair of pink plaster flamingos, a stone statue of a little girl holding out her dress with both hands and a small model windmill. A fleshy yellowish plant spilled out of a ceramic cart drawn by a ceramic donkey.

"Wow," said Audrey. "It's really … interesting."

They both jumped as footsteps crunched on the gravel path. Mavis had come around the side of the house.

"I thought I heard something." She smiled, and Audrey was relieved to see that she had her teeth in. "Come to visit me? That's nice. I've been weeding the veggies out the back and I'm dying for a cuppa. Would you two like a nice lemon squash?"

Audrey looked at Chloe, who shrugged.

"All right," Audrey said. "Thanks."

They followed Mavis into the house. After the brightness outside, it was dark and rather gloomy, with a reek of cigarette smoke. They walked down a long uncarpeted hallway to the kitchen, their footsteps echoing.

"I've got some biscuits, fresh-baked," Mavis said over her shoulder. "You girls like Anzacs?"

"Yes, sure." But even as she said it, Audrey was wishing she hadn't. Now they'd be here forever. Behind her, Chloe deliberately trod on her heel.

The kitchen reminded Audrey of the kitchen in

their old home before they'd had it updated. The floor was worn black-and-white lino tiles, and the cupboards were those old-fashioned ones where you pressed a little knob in the handle to open the door. An old wood stove and a newer electric stove sat together in a chimney nook. On the mantelpiece a wooden clock ticked loudly.

Mavis pulled out a couple of bright green vinyl-padded chairs. "Take a seat." She filled a kettle and put it on the stove, popped a tea bag in a mug that said "World's Best Mum", and then filled two glasses with syrupy yellow cordial and added water from the kitchen tap. She put the glasses on the table next to a round flower-printed tin full of Anzacs, fragrant, golden brown and lacy around the edges.

"Help yourselves." She made her tea, added two heaped teaspoons of white sugar, and took a big ceramic ashtray off the table. "Don't worry, I won't have a ciggie. I never smoke around kids." She sat down, facing them. "What brings you two over here?"

Audrey sipped the cordial. It was delicious, with a strong lemon tang.

"It's your dog. I saw it last night, in our garden.

Mum and Dad said we should tell you. You know, because of the sheep and chooks," she added vaguely.

Mavis looked surprised. "You saw my Daphne? I don't think that's very likely. She always spends the nights here with me." She leaned back in her chair and whistled. "Daphne! Come here, old girl."

There was a slow clicking of claws on the lino, and a very old, very stout blue heeler wandered into the room, bringing with her a strong smell of dog. She licked Mavis's hand and collapsed with a wheeze beside her chair.

Mavis fondled Daphne's ears. "This the dog you saw?"

Audrey shook her head. "No, it was a lot smaller, and it was mostly white. A fox terrier, I think. I only saw it for a few seconds."

"I didn't see it at all," Chloe interrupted, through a mouthful of Anzac. "These biscuits are excellent. Can I please have another?"

Mavis flashed her unnaturally even teeth in a grin. "Have as many as you like. I make good Anzacs – they always sell out at the CWA trading table."

"What's CWA?"

"Country Women's Association. We have a nice

group of ladies, get together every so often. I'll tell your mum about it. She might like to get out now and again."

Audrey decided to pretend she hadn't heard. "The dog I saw must belong to someone else," she said. "Do you know anyone who has a dog like that?"

"Can't say I do. Most people around here have collies and kelpies and such, working dogs. Bill Brewer, who lives up the back of your property, he's got a Rottweiler. He reckons it's not dangerous, but I wouldn't go near it if you paid me. We get a few odd bods around here from time to time. Maybe the little foxy was left up here by someone who didn't want it any more. Some people shouldn't be allowed to have pets."

"But why would it be out at night?" argued Chloe. "My dad said dogs don't get around much at night."

"True." Mavis scratched Daphne's head. "Well, that's it, girls. Can't help you, I'm afraid."

Audrey stood up. "We should go, then. Come on, Chlo."

As they all clumped back down the echoing hallway, Audrey saw a framed picture of birds hanging on the wall. She thought it was a print, maybe cut from a magazine, but when she stopped to look properly she saw that it was an original. Watercolour, most likely. It showed a pair of southern emu-wrens, a male and a female.

"Hey, Mrs–" she started. "I mean ..."

"Call me Mavis. You like my painting?"

"Yes, it's really pretty."

Mavis stood close beside her. She smelled of cigarette smoke, and automatically Audrey moved away a few centimetres. "Beautiful little birds, aren't they?" Mavis said. "There used to be quite a lot of them in this area, but I haven't seen one in years. All that vineyard development saw them off."

"I know, they're endangered. *Stipiturus malachurus*." Audrey realised how nerdy she must sound, how *pretentious*, even to someone old like Mavis. She felt her cheeks grow hot. Behind Mavis's back, Chloe was rolling her eyes.

Mavis beamed. "An expert, eh? We have a local birdwatching group here. We do our bit to raise awareness, or try to. Reckon you might be interested in joining us?"

"Oh ... I don't know." For a second or two she wanted to say yes, she'd love to, but then reality kicked in. *Imagine trekking around the countryside with a lot of old people! What if the kids at school found out?* "Um, maybe one day. Thanks for the drink and the Anzacs."

"Well, don't be strangers. I'm always happy to see visitors. I've got two sons, but they're grown up and living elsewhere, and I don't have any grandkids."

"Sure. See you, Mrs–"

"Mavis. Just call me Mavis."

"*That* wasn't much use," said Chloe, when they were walking back down the road.

"What wasn't?" Audrey was still thinking about the emu-wrens: they looked so fantastic with their long wispy tail feathers. It would be amazing to see one in the wild. She must make a list of local bird species and see if she could find them all …

She pulled her mind back to the present.

"What'd you say, Chlo?"

"The *dog*, bird brain."

"The dog?"

Chloe rolled her eyes again. "The reason we

went to visit Mrs Mavis in the first place. We still don't know whose *dog* it is. I'm starting to think you didn't see anything last night, except maybe Freddy reflected in the window." After a pause, she added, "Her biscuits were really good, though."

CHAPTER 6

But there was a dog.

Audrey saw it again on Sunday when she was walking around the property, notebook in hand, listing the birds she saw and checking for possible nest sites.

She saw it only by accident. She'd seen a parrot (a fabulous crimson rosella, *Platycercus elegans*) flying out of what seemed to be a nest hole in a gum tree, and had swung herself up onto a low branch to check it out. Brilliant! It *was* a nest hole. Empty, probably: it wasn't the breeding season. She'd have to come back later with her torch.

As she turned to scramble down again, she saw a flash of white.

At first she thought it was Freddy. But it wasn't Freddy. It was bigger and sturdier, and now Audrey could see the long muzzle and flopped ears. It was wearing a collar, so it must belong to somebody.

The dog turned and looked at her. Then, as if in answer to a call or a whistle, it sprinted soundlessly away down the paddock, only its head and perky tail visible above the long grass.

Audrey slid down the tree, scraping her legs on the rough bark. She couldn't see the dog anywhere. Where had it gone? If only she hadn't been up the tree! If she'd got hold of the dog, she could have checked to see whether the collar had an address or a phone number on it.

The day was hot and dry. Dad was working in the vineyard, and Mum had driven into town with Chloe to get some things at the supermarket.

Audrey pushed her notebook into her shorts pocket and walked up the hill to the vineyard.

Dad was pulling away weeds at the base of the vines and checking that the irrigation drippers were working. Beneath his broad-brimmed straw hat, his face was shiny with sweat.

"Ah," he said. "Help at last! You can give me a hand, Audrey, if you wouldn't mind. Start at the top row up there and make sure all the drippers are putting water right on the vines. Get rid of any weeds that are in the way. Understood?"

"Sure, understood. Dad, I just saw that dog again. It was over there, at the other end of the paddock. It saw me, but it ran away."

Dad wiped the sweat out of his eyes with the back of his hand. "Very strange," he said. "I wonder who it belongs to."

"Well, that old lady Mavis didn't know about it, and she'd know what's happening around here. She's into everything, birdwatching, CAW ..."

"CWA."

"What you said. It's really weird, though, isn't it? I mean, why is it hanging around our place?"

"Audrey, don't worry about the dog. Get on with what I'm asking you. Please."

"Okay, sorry." Audrey walked further up the hill until she reached the top of the vineyard. She began to move slowly down the first row of vines, checking for evidence of water, pulling out clumps of wiry grass and bindweed. She fixed a piece of irrigation pipe where the dripper had come out altogether, and moved a dripper that was watering a patch of very healthy thistles.

The air was so still she could hear insects moving in the grass. She saw beetles, grasshoppers, a tiny blue skipper butterfly. Above her a whistling kite was hovering, a small dark shape riding on a thermal, its plaintive whistle sliding down to her in a bubble of pure sound.

Haliastur sphenurus.

Audrey gazed into the great upturned blue bowl of the sky. How wonderful it would be to fly! She could feel herself floating effortlessly, the air cool around her body, her outstretched wings barely moving. The world was spread out beneath her like a map in shades of green and brown, every tiny detail crisply outlined and brilliantly clear.

Then the kite swerved and swooped, and she was back to being human again. The sun burned through her T-shirt and the earth was warm beneath her sandalled feet.

The Southern Emu-wren (Stipiturus malachurus) *is a small, shy bird with a tail of six filamentous feathers,* she read. *The body length is 60–70 mm and the tail much longer (90–120 mm). Male: Upperparts are mostly yellowish-brown with blue-grey about the neck and blackish streaks from crown to rump. Underparts are tawny-brown except for the white belly and blue upper breast, throat and eyebrows. Female: Similar in colour, but lacks blue on the breast.*

Audrey looked at the distribution map on the screen of her laptop. Emu-wrens were actually quite widespread. The grey shading extended as far as Western Australia, down to Tasmania and high up the east coast. However, it was described as "uncommon". And locally it was "critically endangered".

Now she thought about it, Audrey felt critically endangered herself. Tomorrow morning was the first day of school. She tried not to think about it.

As it turned out, the kids were a lot like the kids at her old school. There were twenty-five in her class, boys and girls, and they seemed friendly enough. Quite a few of them said hello to her, and a tall fair-haired girl who said her name was Chelsea showed Audrey where her locker was.

The teacher for her grade, Mr Scardino, was a grey-bearded guy who wore socks with health sandals. (Audrey could just imagine what Chloe would say about that.) When the siren went for recess he asked her to stay behind in the classroom for a moment.

"Audrey," he said. "That's a fairly unusual name nowadays, isn't it? Why Audrey?"

"I don't know for sure. I guess my parents just liked it."

"Fans of Audrey Hepburn, perhaps? The film star?"

"Maybe." *And there's no need to say it. She was beautiful, and I don't look a bit like her.*

"Well, Audrey. Tell me about yourself. What subjects do you like best?"

"Um, science, I guess. And maths, a bit."

"Science and maths, eh? I can't tell you how happy that makes me. Why do you like science?"

"I don't know. I … just like finding out about things."

"And which area of science do you find most interesting?"

"Zoology, I guess. Animals. Birds, mainly."

"I see. Any particular aspect of birds?"

"Oh, pretty much everything! I've been interested in them ever since I was little. I want to find out all about them, like how they fly, and why they sing, and how dinosaurs evolved into birds in the first place, and how – why – they are all so different. Like, why are there eagles and hummingbirds and ostriches, but they're all birds? It's sort of like people, although people aren't that different, I guess ..." Her voice trailed off.

Mr Scardino smiled. "Ah, the marvellous theory of evolution," he said. "I have a great fondness for the natural sciences too. Now, how about sport? Here in the country we love our sport. Do you enjoy it?"

I like him, his eyes are kind. "Not so much."

"Play anything?"

"I was in the B netball team at my old school." *And I only made the team because there wasn't anybody else.* "That's all."

"Never mind. Sport isn't everyone's cup of tea, is it? What else are you interested in? Rock climbing, horseriding, music, art?"

"Art, definitely. I'd love to learn how to draw." As she said this, Audrey remembered Mavis's painting of the emu-wrens. It would be great to be able to do something like that! "I'd like to draw birds. You know, properly."

"We have an extremely good art teacher at this school, so your wish may be fulfilled. Let's hope so." He smiled at her again. "Now, have you got any questions about the year ahead? You'll probably find we do some things a little differently here, being a country school."

"How will it be different from the city? I mean, are there special subjects I'll have to study?"

Mr Scardino stroked his beard. "We find that it can be difficult for our non-rural students at first. I'll be organising catch-up milking lessons for you, and I suggest you also take a few optional extras like sheep-herding and elementary bull-wrangling. All very useful skills."

"Really?" A second later Audrey saw the twinkle in his eyes. "Oh. You're joking."

"Me? I never joke." Mr Scardino went to the door and stuck his head out into the corridor.

"Thanks for waiting, girls. Please come in." Two girls came into the classroom, Chelsea and another girl, smaller, slender and dark-haired. Mr Scardino turned to Audrey. "Chel and Huong will look after you and show you the ropes. I'm sure you'll settle in very quickly."

When Mum picked them up in the car, Chloe was bubbling with excitement. She'd made a new best friend already. Her name was Emma, and her mum owned Goosey Gander, that cafe in the main street they'd been to. ("Oh, really?" Mum said, looking interested.) And Chloe had put her name down for tennis, and swimming, and kanga cricket, and there were only nine boys in her class, and her teacher Ms Petersen was really cool, with pink hair and little diamond stars in each ear and a unicorn tattoo on her shoulder.

"And how about you, Audrey?" Mum asked. "Have you got a new best friend too?"

Audrey made a face. "No way. I'm getting to know some of the kids, though. Mr Scardino got two of the girls from my class to look after me, Chelsea and Huong. They seem okay."

"Just okay?"

"I don't know; I haven't got to know them yet. They're nice, I think. At least they don't talk about tractors."

Mum gave her a quizzical look. "Did you expect them to?"

"I didn't know what to expect. Actually they mostly talked about netball, or else they were checking their mobiles like everyone else except me." She gave her mother a meaningful look which, as she expected, was ignored. "Mum, Mr Scardino's really great. I like him a lot."

"I'm glad to hear it. It's important to get on well with your teachers. And I'm glad the day wasn't too much of an ordeal for either of you," said Mum. "That's another hurdle overcome, I suppose." But she didn't say anything else, and neither did Audrey. Chloe, in the back seat, chattered away for most of the trip home.

Freddy trotted out to meet the car as it turned into the driveway.

"Isn't he clever the way he always knows it's us?"

said Chloe. "He's such a smart kitty." The moment she was out of the car she dropped her backpack on the ground and grabbed him, making cooing sounds and cradling him in her arms as she walked towards the house. Audrey picked up her sister's backpack and slung it over her shoulder next to her own.

As Mum went to the boot to get out some bags of groceries, Audrey noticed that her mother's brown hair was beginning to go grey. Immediately she felt a rush of fear. *Mum, please don't be old. I don't want you to be old. Everything's changing, and it's happening so quickly, and I don't want it to change.*

"Pass me one of those bags, Mum," she said. "You shouldn't be carrying heavy stuff. You know you have to be extra careful with your back."

"Nonsense. My back isn't too bad at the moment. And you're loaded up like a packhorse."

"I've got a whole free arm. Give me something." Audrey clicked her fingers. "Come on, I have to look after you."

Mum handed over one of the bags. "Thank you, Audrey. But really, you don't need to look after me at all. It's me who has to look after you two, not the other way round."

"Except Chloe doesn't need much looking after, does she?" Audrey said. "Things always seem to turn out okay for her." She tried not to sound resentful – after all, she loved her little sister. But it was true: Chloe never had to try to fit in, was never afraid of not being liked, was never the last to be picked for a team. "I wish I was more like that."

"Chloe is like Freddy. They'll both always land on their feet. But we're all different, aren't we? You have qualities and talents Chloe doesn't have. Remember that."

"I guess," said Audrey. "Mum?"

"Yes?"

"You haven't landed on your feet yet, have you? Do you think you'll ever like living here?"

"Oh dear, is it that obvious?" Mum laughed, and then looked sad. "It's rather complicated. But perhaps this place can teach us all something. I certainly hope so."

"Me too," Audrey said. She wasn't sure what the farm might teach her, or any of them. But she felt a bit better, a bit more hopeful, as she followed Mum along the path to the back door.

CHAPTER 7

It was Saturday again. Hooray! Not that the week had been all that bad. Audrey decided that she really liked Chel and Huong, and through them she had a foothold in a small, gossipy group of girls who ate their lunch together. She was relieved not to have to suffer the embarrassment of eating alone, and as a useful bonus she learned a lot about her other classmates. Apart from that, school was relatively undemanding, and so far she hadn't been singled out for any unwanted attention. It was as good as she could have expected.

Chloe came home every day with a description of

what Ms Petersen was wearing: yesterday it was the coolest green top with sequins. ("I don't care what she's wearing," Dad said. "What's she teaching you?") And Chloe's new best friend, Emma, had asked her to stay over next weekend. They were going to have dinner in her mum's cafe – so cool, they could have anything at all on the menu. They planned to make popcorn and watch Emma's *Goosebumps* DVD.

"And scare yourselves silly, I suppose," said Mum. "Remember when we watched that old movie *Ghostbusters*, Chlo? You had nightmares for weeks."

Audrey had nothing special to look forward to. Her plans for next weekend were the same as for this one: 1) help Dad with the vines, 2) help Mum in the house and 3) clean out the finch cage.

In the end, working in the vineyard took up nearly all of Saturday. Chloe helped too, for a while, but she was soon bored. She went back to the house, saying she wanted to bake choc-chip cookies with Mum instead.

Audrey stayed with Dad, pulling up weeds and checking drippers, and then she helped him hoist up four large plastic hawk shapes to scare away the starlings that kept pigging out on the ripening grapes. "Starlings are nothing but flying rats," Dad said. "They aren't even native to this country. They shouldn't be here in the first place." Other vineyard owners used bird-scarers that sounded like guns going off every few minutes. It had taken Audrey a while to get used to the sudden loud noises, but now she hardly noticed. Sounds like that had already become part of the normal background to her life.

Sunday brunch was a late lazy meal of sausages and scrambled egg. Chloe was reading *Fantastic Beasts and Where to Find Them*, which she'd borrowed from Emma. Mum was doing the crossword from yesterday's newspaper, and Dad sat calculating what he hoped would be his profit from the grape crop on the back of an envelope. Freddy lay stretched out in a slice of warm sunlight beside the back door.

Audrey didn't feel like reading, but she had nothing else to do except homework, and she wasn't quite ready to do *that*. It would be school tomorrow, and all she'd done was work with Dad or waste time. The memory of the distant shadow in the rocks came into her mind, teasing her with its mystery. The more she thought about it, the more she longed to find out what it was. A quick look, that was all she wanted. How could it hurt? Nobody needed to know. And even if they did, who would care?

"You want to go exploring?" she asked Chloe. "We could see if there really is a cave down the creek. You know, near that crooked tree."

"Why? You didn't want to, before."

"I do now."

"You'll be trespassing."

"I know." *Why do I want to see it so much?*

Chloe narrowed her eyes. "You'll probably just stop about a thousand times to look at insects or something. I'm staying here. I want to finish my book."

"Your loss," said Audrey. She raised her voice. "I'm going for a walk, Mum."

Mum looked up from her crossword. "Don't be long," she said. "And watch out for snakes."

"Sure." Audrey dropped a kiss on her mother's head as she left.

The sun was still high in the sky. On the hill paddock waves of pale grass shimmered, stretching away like a billowing sea. Bees in a blossoming gum tree hummed. The ducks on the dam rose from the water in a flurry of wings, their quacking sounding like hoarse laughter.

When Audrey was halfway across the paddock, she stopped.

The dog had appeared silently in front of her. Where had it come from?

Audrey squatted and stretched out her hand. "Here, boy!" She clicked her tongue.

The dog turned and looked at her, then started to trot away down the hill, towards the creek. After a moment it stopped and turned its head again.

Audrey laughed. "You want me to follow you?"

The little dog seemed to laugh back at her. It was moving quickly now, and Audrey had to jog to keep up. The dog led her straight to the boundary fence, and disappeared.

How did it get through? Audrey couldn't see a gap anywhere. But if the dog had got through, there must be a way.

She looked at the fence more closely, and then pushed aside some tall dry grass to find quite a large gap, close to the ground, where the chicken wire had been bent upward. *Yes!* She slithered through on her back, taking care not to tear her clothes.

The rocky creek bed wound away ahead of her, a string of drying puddles fringed with reeds. But where was the dog?

"Here, boy!" she called again.

And there it was, closer than she'd expected. It was standing on a large rock, gazing at her with liquid brown eyes.

The dog bounded off down the creek bed. Audrey ran after it, stumbling on the rocks. There was a clatter of loose stones, and a thud as she landed on her bottom. *Ouch!* There was no way she could keep up with the dog. And now it had gone again. How could it do that? One second it was there, the next it had vanished.

Audrey scrambled to her feet, and wondered what to do.

A gust of wind whirled around her, rustling the reeds. The crooked tree was only a few metres away. It grew among rocks, its roots at eye level.

Yip! Yip!

The barking sounded very near.

Audrey walked forward, step by careful step – and there it was.

The entrance was a narrow gap in the rocks. The dog stood just outside it, wagging his tail. He had a pleased, alert look.

"Wow!" Audrey said aloud. "I *knew* there was a cave!"

The dog turned and scampered away into the shadows. His white body glimmered for a second, and then disappeared again.

Audrey sniffed: she could smell a trace of smoke. Not cigarette smoke, but cooking smoke, like a barbecue. Could someone be in the cave? She hadn't thought of that.

Her mind raced. What if it was a feral, or (worse) a drug addict, or (even worse) someone on the run from the police?

Once again she felt that there was something strange about this place, something warning her to keep away. But the pull towards it was stronger. Perhaps whoever was in the cave needed help. Could that be why the dog had brought her here?

Go home, her careful self told her. *You have no idea what sort of person could be in that cave. It could be someone really dangerous. Go home now.*

But I've walked all this way! argued her braver

self. *And I want to see what's inside it.*

You know what Mum would say, warned her careful self.

Of course her braver self knew what Mum would say, but … *I'll have a really, really quick look. If it's scary, I'll just run away.*

Her heart beating crazily, she squeezed into the cave entrance.

The narrow tunnel was less than two metres long. It opened out into a low chamber. And inside–

Audrey stared.

CHAPTER 8

On a flat rock in the middle of the cave chamber a candle, wedged into a bottle, burned with a long tapering flame. Someone was living here: Audrey could see an enamel mug, a suitcase with things spilling out of it, the ashy remains of a fire. The dog was lying on what looked like a heap of blankets.

Shadows leaped and wavered.

At first the cave seemed empty, apart from the dog, and Audrey was both relieved and disappointed. Then, away from the light, at the back of the cave, she made out a darker shadow. A human-sized shape. Her heart thumped.

The shape stood up, became a person, moved towards her.

"Get out! This is private property!" It was a male voice.

"I'm sorry – I just wanted–"

"Hop it."

"I didn't mean–"

"*Get out!*"

"Sorry," Audrey said again. Fear was making her hands sweat. She wiped them on her jeans. "I didn't know anyone was here, but your dog–"

The boy – he was only a boy – came a little closer. In the candlelight his face was all hollows and angles. "What about my dog?"

"We've seen him around our place, and we thought he was a stray," Audrey said, the words coming out in a rush. "Then, when I saw him again today, it was kind of like he wanted me to follow him, so I did, and I ended up here."

"Oh." The boy was still wary. "You're on your own?"

"Yes." What was this boy doing in the cave? He didn't seem to be very old, maybe fifteen, or even younger. He was wearing what looked like a school uniform – long pants and a light-coloured shirt with the sleeves partly rolled up.

"And … you're only here because of my dog?"

"He was in our garden the other night," Audrey said. At last her heart was beginning to slow down. "He scared our cat."

"Ah." The boy grinned now, a slow grin, half his mouth quirking upwards. "Snowy's not too keen on cats." He spoke with a distinctive country drawl, like a lot of the kids in Audrey's class at school.

"I guess not," said Audrey. "Our cat wasn't too keen on him either."

"Hope the little bloke didn't make a nuisance of himself."

Audrey shook her head. "We just didn't know where he'd come from."

In the dim light the boy's face was mask-like. "Sorry if I was rude," he said. "It's just that–" He stopped.

"Just that … what?"

The boy didn't reply. He sat down beside the dog, which moved to rest its head on his thigh. "I don't think I've seen you before," he said. "You live around here?"

"We've got the farm further down the creek." Audrey waved her hand vaguely in that direction.

"What, the Keppler place?"

"Yes, that's the people who owned it before us." There was nothing at all threatening about this boy, she decided. Earlier he'd been like a male pigeon, puffing up his feathers before a fight, trying to make himself look bigger. "So what are you doing in this cave?"

The boy looked at her intently. "If I tell you, you've got to promise not to tell anyone I'm here."

Audrey nodded. "Sure, I promise."

"Can I trust you?"

"I'm actually very good at keeping secrets. Really."

There was such a deep silence that Audrey could hear the blood beating in her ears. Then the boy said, "You'd better take a seat then. And you could tell us your name."

There was nothing to sit on, so Audrey lowered herself to the cave floor. It was cold and gritty. "I'm Audrey."

"*Audrey*? That's a girl's name."

"That would be because I'm a girl."

"Well, I'll be. I thought you were a boy."

"Oh. Well, I'm not."

"In that case, I beg your pardon." The boy grinned again. "Nice to meet you, Audrey. I'm Ross Finch. My mates call me Finch."

"Hi, Finch." Audrey gazed around the cave. "So … *do* you live here?"

"Yeah."

"Been here long?"

"About two weeks."

"Wow, that's amazing." *How could anyone live in a cave for two weeks?* "So do you go to school here? I mean, did you?" She hesitated. Wasn't it illegal to skip school? Maybe she shouldn't have mentioned it.

Finch didn't seem at all concerned, though. "I used to. Then I started working for my uncle. Bill Brewer, you know him?"

Audrey remembered what Mavis had said about Bill Brewer. "That's the guy who has the farm behind us," she said. "The one with the big dog."

Finch nodded. "Yeah, he's got a dog. Big black thing with a nasty temper. I wasn't sorry to say goodbye to *him* when I quit my job and came here."

"Why'd you quit your job?"

"Just … reasons."

"Is that why you're living here?"

"Yes."

"Oh." While Audrey was wondering what to say next, Finch spoke again.

"I never knew the Keppler place was up for sale."

"We haven't been there long." Audrey realised that it was ages since she'd thought about her old life. "We used to live in the city, but my dad lost his job."

"That's too bad," Finch said. "I reckoned you had to be a city kid, the way you talk and that. Got any brothers or sisters?"

"I've got a sister, Chloe. She's ten, younger than me. What about you?"

"There's four of us." Immediately Audrey heard the change in his voice: he sounded warmer, more sure of himself. "I'm the oldest. There's me, then there's Pete, he's twelve, then Lizzy, who's ten, then little May. I haven't seen them in a while, not since they moved away from here with Mum and Dad. Gee, I miss those kids."

Audrey tried to imagine not living with Chloe. They didn't always get along, but how she would miss her little sister! It would be like losing a part of herself. "You'll see them again, won't you?"

"Well, I don't plan on stopping here forever. And I've got Snowy. He's my best mate, no question. If anything happened to Snowy I don't know what I'd do. Pack it in, most likely."

"Why should anything happen to him?"

"There's plenty of risks for dogs in the country – snakes, mainly. And fox baits."

"What's fox baits?"

"You *are* a city kid, aren't you? Baits are poisoned meat you put out to kill foxes. Foxes'll eat anything. The trouble is, so will dogs."

The candle flame flickered and began to sink. The cave grew darker. Audrey said, "Where do you get food from? Sorry about all the questions. But if you don't want people to know you're here I guess you can't just go down to the bakery for a loaf of bread."

"I do pretty well. I have to go out after it's dark, but there's always eggs from chook houses, and no one misses a few plums or tomatoes. And I trap rabbits. I nicked a couple of traps from my uncle, along with some candles and matches and a few other things."

Once again Finch grinned his slow, lopsided grin. "I've got to be careful I don't get caught, though. If anyone dobbed me in to Uncle Bill, he'd hand me over to the cops." He stroked Snowy's head. "And what would we do then, hey, boy?"

The candle flame guttered and died, and the air in the cave felt thick and heavy. It seemed that as far as Finch was concerned, the conversation was at an end.

Audrey stood up and brushed the grit off her legs. "I should go now. I told Mum I wouldn't be long." She hesitated. "Um – can I come round after school tomorrow?" *Did I really say that?*

Silence.

"Would that be okay?" *What if he says no? I'll die.*

"Yeah, I'd like that. It's been good to talk."

"Do you need anything? I could bring you stuff."

"Thanks, but I'm right."

"See you tomorrow, then."

Audrey thought she saw Finch raise a hand in farewell, but in the darkness she couldn't be sure.

CHAPTER 9

Walking out of the stuffy cave was like walking into instant air conditioning. The sun shone brilliantly, a breeze cooled Audrey's hot face and the sounds of the outside world came alive again.

She picked her way back along the creek bed, thinking about Finch. *I just talked to a boy who is living in a cave. How amazing is that?* She repeated the words to herself: *A boy. Living. In. A. Cave.* It still didn't seem real.

Her brain buzzed, unable to settle.

"Unbelievable," she said aloud.

Finch seemed quite friendly, but at the same

time there was something kind of weird about him. Could he be on drugs? Audrey considered that for a moment, but decided it wasn't likely, and in any case she didn't know enough to be able to tell. (How *did* you tell?) He was definitely tense, though – like a wild bird, poised for flight at any moment.

There has to be something I can do to help him, she thought. *He shouldn't be living in a cave, for a start. You can tell he misses his family really badly. Don't the Salvos look after homeless people? Surely his uncle wouldn't report him to the police just because he stole some food.*

Then again … maybe Finch thought living in a cave was fun. Maybe it *was* fun. It would be like camping, except not in a tent. She'd been camping once, with her family, but it had been a disaster. It had rained almost the whole time and their camp fire went out and they'd had to drive about a hundred ks to the next town to buy fish and chips. Dad had been in the worst mood.

At least she'd solved the mystery of the dog, except now she couldn't tell anybody. Oh God, she was *dying* to tell Chloe! "But I mustn't," she reminded herself. "I promised." She kept on walking. *He has a nice face, at least what I could see of it. There wasn't too much light. I could see his eyes, though. I like blue eyes. I wish mine were blue. And he's really polite.* Most boys weren't polite. Audrey had been ignored or teased by a lot of boys at St Cuthbert's.

Finch had said, "It's been good to talk". He must be lonely.

Audrey knew how it felt to be lonely.

As soon as she opened the back door, she heard voices.

Mum and Mavis were sitting at the kitchen table with two mugs and a plate of assorted cream biscuits between them. Chloe was sitting at the other end, carefully colouring in a complicated design with textas.

They all looked up at Audrey as she walked in, and Mum frowned. "You were gone a long time, Audrey. I was starting to think something had happened to you."

Audrey went to the fridge and poured herself a glass of milk. "Sorry, Mum."

"I thought I'd come over to see if you'd solved the mystery of the little dog," Mavis said. "Been racking my brains to think where he might've come from. You find out anything?"

Audrey gulped her milk. It was like Mavis could see into her mind. She answered without looking at her. "No, we never found out any more. He must be a stray."

"Did you see him again after that first time?"

"No."

Mum interrupted. "Oh, that's not true, Audrey."

For a moment, Audrey panicked. *How could Mum know?*

Mum went on: "Remember, you said you saw him in the paddock the other day."

That was close. "Oh yes, sorry, I forgot. I tried to follow him but he ran away."

Mavis looked at her curiously. "I hope the little fella's all right. It's not so easy for dogs on the loose. Cats'll always find themselves a feed somewhere."

"He looked okay."

Freddy wandered into the kitchen, sized up the opportunities, and leaped on to Mavis's lap. He gazed up at her, blinked, and started to purr loudly.

Mavis chuckled. "Amazing how cats always go straight for the person who doesn't like them."

"But that's *Freddy*!" said Chloe. "You can't say you don't like Freddy!"

Mavis gently but firmly eased Freddy to the floor. "I'm sure he's a nice enough cat, as cats go. I just can't stand the creatures. Nothing more than killing machines. I like birds, and birds and cats don't mix."

Chloe picked Freddy up and hugged him. "Fred's not like other cats. He doesn't need to hunt for food. And we always keep him inside at night so he can't hurt anything. He's.never caught a bird, not ever."

"Well, that's a real good start," said Mavis, "but once a cat, always a cat. Killing's in their nature." She turned to Audrey. "I was wondering if you'd like to come to our next birdwatchers' outing next Saturday." She pronounced it "Sat-dee". "We leave from the post office at nine o'clock sharp. Your mum and dad could come too if they want. We're going up to the range to see if we can spot some yellow-tailed black cockatoos."

Audrey could see Chloe looking at her with a peculiar expression on her face. She nearly choked on her milk. "Thanks, Mrs–"

"Mavis."

"Thanks, but I can't." She looked down at the table. "I've got – I've got netball practice on Saturday."

"Oh, are you playing netball, Aud?" Chloe asked in her sweetest voice. "I didn't know you'd tried out for the team."

"I forgot to tell you."

"Not to worry." Mavis gave Audrey an understanding look, and she had the uncomfortable feeling that the old woman had seen straight through her feeble lie. "I just thought you might be interested. Well, thanks for the tea and bickies, Caroline. I'd best be off. I promised my brother I'd look in on him before tea."

"Nice of you to drop by. And if we hear anything more about the dog we'll let you know."

"I'd appreciate it. Goodbye all. I'll see myself out."

As soon as the screen door had banged shut behind her, Audrey turned to Chloe, her face furious. "Thanks for that. I'm just starting to get used to school. You know what it'd be like for me if anyone knew I was going birdwatching with a bunch of old people."

"You don't know that at all, Audrey," said Mum. "You girls judge everything by how it looks to others, don't you?"

"Mum, you're just as bad. I saw your face when you were stuck here with Mavis."

Mum's cheeks turned pink. "Nonsense. I – to be honest, I'm not keen on people I don't know well dropping in at all hours. Especially when we don't have a lot to talk about."

"That doesn't matter with Mavis," Chloe said. "She does all the talking."

"Very true." Mum got up and began to clear away the mugs and plates. "I suppose she's quite a nice old thing, really. And we can do with a few friends out here, can't we?"

CHAPTER 10

"I'm going for a walk down the creek, Mum!" yelled Audrey. It was after school on Monday, and Mum was in what she called "the office" but was really a tiny lean-to sleep-out at the side of the house.

"Be careful!" yelled Mum.

"I will!"

"Don't forget your homework!"

"I won't!"

Chloe bounced out of her bedroom. "Can I come too?"

Audrey thought quickly. "I'm not going far. I just want to check out the creek, see if there are any tadpoles yet."

"Oh. Forget it, then." Chloe stared at her. "Why are you wearing that dress? You haven't worn that in ages."

"I spilled juice on my school uniform, okay?"

Chloe shrugged. "Whatever." She stared harder. "Did you know you're getting a pimple? It's on your chin, right there." She pointed.

"I did. Thanks for reminding me."

"No worries."

As Audrey headed for the door, she heard Mum's voice again. "Watch out for snakes!"

When she reached the cave, Audrey hung back, uncertain. Even from the outside, the cave felt empty. It was almost like ... like someone had died. But that was stupid, of course.

"Finch!" she called. "Are you there?"

Not a sound, not a movement.

"Can I come in?" She almost added, "Are you decent?", which was what Dad always said before he came into her bedroom. She stifled a nervous urge to giggle. "I'm coming in, okay?"

As she made her way slowly down the entrance to the cave, head bent, Snowy skittered towards her. He crouched and wagged his tail, but retreated quickly when she put out a hand to pat him.

Audrey took a few more steps. "Finch?" she called. "It's me!"

A bud of light glowed in the dark.

"G'day!" came Finch's voice.

Audrey emerged from the tunnel into the chamber. When her eyes adjusted to the dimness, she saw Finch sitting at the back of the cave, Snowy curled up at his feet.

Finch was making something. She could hear the scrape of a knife against wood or stone.

"Hi." Audrey moved shyly into the circle of light. Would Finch notice that she was wearing a dress? She sat on the ground, first carefully tucking her skirt around her legs. "I'm glad you're still here. For a minute I thought you might've gone."

"Not a chance," Finch said. "Here, have a look at this. I'm making it for May, my little sister. She'll be seven in a few weeks. The wood's from an old dead walnut tree I spotted a few days ago. It's a nice timber, walnut."

He held up what he was working on. "There's still a few details to sort out, but I'm getting there."

Audrey saw a small roundish wooden bird. The shape was complete, and there were carved hints of wings and feathers.

"It's a finch!" she exclaimed. "That's amazing! You're really clever!"

Finch looked pleased. "They have a particular sort of body, don't they, finches? Little fat things with short tails. I thought May would like it, being as how she's a Finch, you know, same as me." He returned to his carving. "She's a little fat thing too, but she wouldn't be happy to hear me say it."

"I've got finches at home," Audrey told him. "Zebras. I've had them a while, and there's only five left now. They're quite old."

"Cage birds?"

"Yes. They were all hatched in the cage."

"You feel sorry for them, don't you?" Finch said, working away at the shaping of a folded wing. "It's like they're in prison. There's all that great big sky to fly in, and they'll never know what it feels like."

"I know," Audrey said. "But my finches wouldn't

survive outside the cage. If I let them go, they'd die. I try to keep them happy. I do care about them."

"I'm sure you're real good to them," Finch said. "The point is, wild birds should stay wild. We shouldn't interfere with nature, it upsets the balance." He looked over at her. "Have you ever heard of the passenger pigeon?"

"No. Should I?"

"I read about them in a magazine a while ago. Last century there were billions of passenger pigeons in North America. Seems the flocks were so big that when they were on the wing they blotted out the sun. But people cut down the forests they lived in, and farmers shot them because they ate their crops, and they were killed for food, and now they're extinct. Out of all those billions of birds, there's not one left."

"Not one?"

"Not a single one. It's a real shocker, isn't it? And what about the dodo? It was a kind of pigeon too, a big one, and it was good to eat. Or it was. Nobody alive has ever seen one. People hunted it, and because it couldn't fly – it only had tiny little wings – it was a sitting duck." He laughed. "Sorry, that was accidental, honestly. I didn't mean to joke about the poor old dodo."

"I've only ever seen drawings of the dodo in *Alice in Wonderland*. I always thought it wasn't real." Audrey hugged her knees. "You know a lot, don't you?"

"I read a bit. I like knowing things."

"Me too," Audrey said. She paused. "Actually, I want to be a scientist. A zoologist. I want to study birds." She waited for the expected silence, or a look of disbelief.

"Well, good on you. You must be real brainy. I didn't think girls cared much about science and that."

"Actually, lots of girls care."

"I suppose I don't know enough girls." Finch grinned his lopsided grin. "I'm glad I know you, though."

Audrey let the words stay in her mind, savouring their warmth. Then, because she felt that maybe now they knew each other well enough, she said, as if the thought had just come to her, "You know, you don't have to stay here, Finch. If you want to be with your family, my parents would help you."

Immediately she noticed the change in him. He put down the little wooden bird and leaned back against the cave wall, retreating into darkness.

"Thanks, but I don't need any help," he said. His eyes glittered. "I know what I'm doing, and I can be a lot more use to my old man if I keep away. The last thing he wants is another mouth to feed."

"But he's your *father*," argued Audrey. "I mean, how d'you think he'd feel if he knew where you were? And your mum – wouldn't she be worried?"

"You have to understand how it was," Finch said. "Things weren't too good for us when we were living here. My dad was out of work for a while, so when a mate offered him a job at the abattoirs, of course he had to take it. That's why the family moved away."

"So why didn't you go with them?" Audrey asked. She felt braver now. In for a penny, in for a pound – that's what Mum would have said. And it seemed that Finch wanted to talk, or needed to.

"By then I was working for Uncle Bill. He said he'd look after me, and he'd let me keep Snowy. We all agreed to it. So Mum and Dad and the kids left, and I stayed. That's it."

"But … your job didn't work out?"

"No. Best I don't talk about that, though."

"Why?"

"Uncle Bill is my mum's brother."

"So?"

"I don't want Mum to be upset. You know how things get around."

"I wouldn't tell anyone. I *won't* tell anyone. Cross my heart."

There was a long silence before Finch began to speak again. "Uncle Bill wasn't … well, he wasn't what we thought he was," he said. "One of my jobs was looking after his pigs. I don't mind looking after pigs – you can get quite fond of a pig – but my uncle fed those pigs better than he fed me. Then he started belting me. Not all the time, but when he'd had a few drinks he'd go crook at me for the smallest thing.

"One day he put the boot into Snowy, and that was it. No one hurts my dog. What happened was, Snowy thought he'd try and stop Uncle Bill from bashing me. He's a game little bloke – barked his head off, bit my uncle in the leg and got a good kicking as a reward. He could've got himself killed. I wouldn't put anything past Uncle Bill when he's red-eyed mean. So I decided that Snowy and I had better get out of there fast. The only problem was, I had no money."

"Why? Didn't your uncle pay you?"

"You don't pay family, according to Uncle Bill. I got my board and lodging. More or less."

"That's just *wrong*," said Audrey. "Why didn't you—"

"It was my problem, right? So it was up to me to sort it out. I reckoned the best thing I could do was disappear for a bit. I've always known about this cave, it's on old Frank Blix's property, but he's ninety not out and he wouldn't have been here in years. So one night I got my things together and walked out. I left a note for Uncle Bill telling him I was going back to my family."

"What if your uncle talks to your mum? If they talk to each other they'll soon find out you aren't where you're supposed to be."

"It's not that likely. They don't get in touch too often."

"All right, but there must be better places to live than a cave," Audrey persisted. "There's the Salvos, for a start. They have hostels where you can stay, don't they? Or else, I know you don't want to go to the police, but they'd help, I know they would–"

"The police? Not on your life." Finch sounded annoyed now. "Look, I'm fine. I don't need the cops sticking their noses in, or anyone else. And I promise you I'm not going back to Uncle Bill."

"Sorry," Audrey said humbly. "I didn't mean to interfere. I only wanted to help."

"I appreciate that. Thanks." Finch picked up the little wooden bird and began to work on it again. After a while he said, "You know, there's something about this place. I reckon there's been plenty of other people living here before me, Aboriginal people and that. It feels as if … as if people have always found shelter here, over hundreds or maybe thousands of years. Sometimes I can feel them all around me – at night, mostly. It's hard to explain, but I know they're there."

Audrey shivered. "That's so weird. What are they like? Are they spooky or friendly?"

"They're pretty friendly. Well, they've looked after me so far."

"I don't think I'd like being with people I couldn't see. And I'd hate not having a bathroom, or a proper bed, or any windows … and don't you get lonely? I'd be so lonely!"

"I'm not lonely – I've got Snowy. He's as good a mate as you could wish for." He bent forward to stroke the little dog. "And as for not having a bathroom, there's a waterhole not too far away, plenty of water for me to have a wash and fill the billy. If you go down there around sunrise, the place is filled with birds. It's magic." He turned towards her, his face barely visible in the candle's glow. "Hey, you like birds. You should come to the waterhole with me one morning."

Audrey felt her heart thump, and then beat faster. "Really?"

"Why not?"

"I might do that. I mean, yes, I'd like to. Thanks."

There was a glint of teeth in the darkness as Finch smiled. "And you can stop worrying about me. You'd be surprised how easy it is to live rough. The truth is, this is a special place. I like it here. I feel safe."

CHAPTER 11

"Mr Scardino?"

"Yes, Audrey?"

"Can I ask you something? Sorry, I know it's nearly time for class–"

"Don't worry about that. Fire away."

"Mr Scardino, were there ever Aboriginal people living around here? You know, before white people took over?'

"Took over is right, Audrey. A tragic business, as we now know, although at the time the settlers felt differently. But yes, at one time I believe there were many Indigenous people in this district."

"It's just – I mean, there's this cave, and a friend of mine says he thinks people might have lived in it ages ago. Aboriginal people."

Mr Scardino raised his eyebrows. "Oh? Where is this cave?"

"I'm not sure. I haven't actually seen it." *Liar.*

"I understand there are one or two caves in the area, but I can't be sure they were ever inhabited by Indigenous people. Mostly they made bark shelters and the like. They used hollow gum trees as shelters, too. But I suppose a cave, if it was big enough, could have made a suitable home."

"Oh." *I wish I could tell him about Finch. I want to tell someone so badly.* "Mr Scardino?"

"Audrey."

"Would it be safe to live in a cave?"

"It would depend. Not the warmest or most comfortable of places, I'd say, particularly in winter. And I suppose there could be hazards like rockfalls, or floods, depending on what sort of cave it was and where it was situated." He glanced at his watch. "Why the sudden interest in caves?"

"Oh, no reason. Except I just met this person who, um, knew about this cave and thought Aboriginal people might have lived there once. That's all."

"I see."

"Mr Scardino, how old do you have to be before you can leave school?"

Mr Scardino looked startled. "I hope you're not asking for yourself, Audrey. I would expect you to stay at school until Year Twelve, and then–"

"Sorry, no, it's not about me. I'm asking for my friend, he's the same friend who, um, knows about the cave."

"Well, in this state you are legally required to continue your school education until you are sixteen, and if you leave school at sixteen you must complete your education by enrolling in some other form of training until you are seventeen."

"So you can't leave school until you're sixteen? Do people ever leave when they're younger than that?"

"Sometimes, I suppose, if there's a very good reason, but these days people generally appreciate the need to complete their education." Mr Scardino looked up as the siren went for the start of classes. "Why don't you take your seat, Audrey? The hordes will descend any minute. Get your maths books out."

Audrey went to her desk, feeling elated because she'd managed to sort of talk about Finch without actually mentioning him. Sharing him even the tiniest bit with Mr Scardino made him seem more real. Whenever she thought about him, which was nearly all the time, he seemed further and further away from her. She had to keep trying to grab him back.

Was Finch really sixteen? Audrey was surprised. He didn't look that old, although it was hard to tell with boys. One boy she knew at St Cuthbert's had looked about nine when he was actually twelve, while another boy, hardly any older, was already shaving.

All through the lesson she tried to concentrate on maths, but kept coming back to what Finch had said yesterday. She couldn't quite remember his exact tone of voice. *You must come to the waterhole with me one morning.* (Was that it? Was it "must" or "should"?) He hadn't actually said which morning, but Audrey had already worked out that Sunday, very early, would be the best time to go. Chloe would be sleeping over at Emma's, and Mum and Dad usually got up late on Sunday. Would it be a totally dumb thing to take Finch up on the invitation? Did he really mean it? What if he was only being polite?

She wished she could make his life easier, but he seemed terribly independent. In a way – and this thought shocked her a little – he reminded her of Mavis. It must be that country thing.

She couldn't wait to see him again.

All through the week the weather grew hotter. An Indian summer, Mum called it, because it was actually autumn now and it should have been getting cooler. The farmhouse wasn't air conditioned, and although there was a ceiling fan in the living room, all it did was push the warm air around. To make things worse, it was very humid, but it didn't rain. Mum refused to cook, and just put out cold meat and salad for dinner. Mavis's cucumbers had found a natural home on the compost heap. Freddy lost all interest in food and flopped wherever he could find a cool place.

Audrey and Chloe went to school, came home, and mooched around the house, moaning that they were too hot to do anything. ("So much for those fantastic thick walls, Dad," Chloe said.)

"It's climate change," Dad said. "We're going to get more and more of this weather. My grapes are almost ready to be picked, and the whole crop could be ruined. The birds are having a field day already."

Mum frowned. "Ian, I thought the hawk scarecrows you'd rigged up were solving that problem?"

"Not entirely," Dad said. "Those starlings are cunning little devils, and now the lorikeets are having a feast as well. I've only got four hawks up, and I need more for the size of the vineyard. Next year I'll go for the gun scarer."

"You'll have to get help for the picking," said Mum. "You know I can't do anything, not with my back. And before you suggest it, I'm not having either of the girls skip school."

"I don't mind missing school," Audrey said. "A day or two won't hurt."

"No," said Mum. "No, no and no."

Audrey didn't argue. She was still having doubts about her plan to go to the waterhole at dawn on Sunday. It could be the worst idea ever. Finch seemed friendly enough, but he was a *boy*. What did she really know about him? What if (horrible thought) he thought she was *interested* in him? She'd overheard older boys at St Cuthbert's talking about girls, usually less pretty girls, who *came on* to boys – sluts, they called them. Audrey hated the ugly sound of it. Would Finch think she was a slut?

Finch isn't like that, she told herself. *He's nice. He's … respectful.* (He'd said, "I beg your pardon.") And going out so early in the morning would be an adventure. She'd never seen the sun rise before.

What did she have to lose? It wasn't like she was going on a *date*, for heaven's sake.

On Saturday, Chloe was all ready for her sleepover hours early, and then changed her clothes at least half-a-dozen times before she was satisfied. She'd braided her hair with ribbons, and she was wearing a jangle of thin coloured bracelets on each arm. Emma's parents came to pick her up in their Land Rover. Emma's mum was tall and elegant, and she was wearing white jeans and a pair of embroidered flat shoes with sparkly bits. Audrey could see that Chloe was impressed. She took fashion very seriously.

Chloe and Emma vanished into Chloe's bedroom while Mum and Dad sat with Emma's parents at the table on the back verandah and shared a bottle of white wine. Audrey sat with them for a while, but she soon grew tired of listening to their conversation about chefs and menus, and Mum had only put out a small bowl of olives, so there wasn't even anything good to eat. As soon as she could, she got up and went over to the birdcage to check on her finches.

The little birds seemed unusually quiet. *It must be this hot weather*, Audrey thought. Then she saw a bundle of pale feathers lying very still in a corner of the cage.

As soon as she opened the hatch, there was a panicked flurry of fluttering and loud cheeping. She reached inside, picked Gummo up and held him gently. His body was so light she could barely feel it in her hand. The bright red beak was still now, the eyes closed, the tiny claws limp. One wing had lost half its pinion feathers.

Audrey felt a great wave of sadness. Poor Gummo. What had been the point of his life? He'd been in prison since the moment he was hatched. Because he was at the bottom of the pecking order he'd been constantly bullied. In the animal world he hadn't served any important or necessary function. He'd just been alive – no more.

Now that his body had been removed, his four cage mates were cheeping and flitting about as if nothing had happened. He mattered no more to them than a single millet seed in their feed bowl.

"But he *did* matter," Audrey said to herself. "*I* cared about him."

She wiped her eyes and blew her nose. Then she went to the shed, found a spade and buried Gummo in the front garden, near to where she'd seen Snowy all those nights ago.

Dinner that night was quiet without Chloe. Nobody talked much. Dad made some comment about how well Goosey Gander must be doing, but he said it in a way that meant he was really envious, and felt that Emma's parents hadn't worked hard enough, or maybe suffered enough, to deserve it. After that he seemed depressed, even though there was mango for dessert – his favourite.

Audrey said goodnight to Mum and Dad at nine o'clock, her usual bedtime, and then lay on her bed and read. She'd set her alarm for six o'clock. That would give her plenty of time to get to the cave. It was still daylight saving, which meant that the sun would rise at about seven o'clock – she'd googled that on her laptop to make sure. At the same time she couldn't resist logging on to Instagram to see what Jaz was up to. Already Jaz seemed to her like a character in a book, someone from a different world. And there she was, another selfie in a cafe, but this time she was with somebody. A boy! They had their heads together, cheek to cheek, and they were sharing a drink with two straws. Audrey sat back in her chair, surprised. Although really there was no need to be surprised: Jaz had always talked about wanting to have a boyfriend. *Me and Charlie & a COOOOL ice coffee*, read the caption. It was followed by two emojis, a smiley face and a heart. Twenty-three people "liked" the post, and there were two comments: *Are you 2 in luv?* and *your so cooool Jaz xx* with a rose emoji.

She shut down the laptop and picked up her book again, but she couldn't concentrate. Instead she started to worry about what she was wearing.

Should she choose something more girly, a bit prettier? Would Finch even notice? In the end she decided on her butterfly T-shirt rather than the plain white one, and her new jeans. She'd already secretly borrowed one of Chloe's sequined headbands.

She stared at herself in the mirror and dabbed concealer on her pimple, which seemed bigger than ever. She combed her hair, put on Chloe's headband and took it off again. It didn't look right after all – her hair was too short. If only Chloe was there to tell her what to do! Chloe always knew what worked and what didn't. It was a gift, Mum said: something you were born with. Audrey knew it was a gift she didn't have.

She couldn't stop thinking about Jaz and that boy, Charlie. She didn't think he went to St Cuthbert's, unless he was new there. Jaz had probably met him when she was on holidays or something. They must know each other really well to be sharing a drink like that.

At ten o'clock she lay down on her bed, fully dressed apart from her sneakers, and switched off her bedside lamp. Mum and Dad were in bed now: she could hear them talking quietly, and their bedroom light showed in a bright line beneath her closed door. After a few minutes the light disappeared. Soon Dad started to snore.

Audrey didn't sleep. She couldn't. When the glowing red figures of her alarm clock moved to 6.00, she got up and put on her sneakers. She walked softly down the hallway, not even stopping to stroke Freddy, who had wandered out of the kitchen to see what was going on.

She opened the back door carefully, slipped outside and closed the door with the tiniest of clicks.

The moon was low on the horizon, but the sky was still dense with stars. All the daytime colours had drained away: the grass was grey, the vineyard black. The trees were motionless, their dark leaves hanging.

As she walked down the hill paddock, Audrey felt a bubble of excitement rising in her chest.

CHAPTER 12

A quarter of an hour later, she was standing outside the entrance to the cave. But night had changed the personality of the place. Now it was cold, brooding.

Audrey hugged herself, wishing she'd worn a jumper. Suddenly she remembered Gummo, the stillness of his tiny body, all that life gone.

Don't think about it.

"Finch?" she called.

A tiny wind gusted, blowing grit against her legs. The air lifted and sank, and in that fraction of a moment she heard stone chinking against stone. She raised her eyes to the sound. And there on a steep rock, silhouetted against the starry sky, were the black shapes of a boy and a dog.

The shapes disappeared, and a few seconds later Audrey saw Finch walking towards her down the dry creek bed. Beside him, his white feet twinkling over the stones, was Snowy.

"Finch!" Relief made Audrey speak more loudly than usual. "It's me!"

Finch sounded cool and distant. "G'day! What are you doing here?"

Audrey's stomach contracted. *He's forgotten. He doesn't want to see me.* "Sorry. I should've told you. You asked me if I wanted to go to the waterhole with you, so … here I am." She took a couple of steps forward, and then stopped. She didn't want to look like an overeager little kid.

"You want to see the birds, right?"

"Yes. Please …" *This isn't how I imagined it. I'm such an idiot. I should go home.* She felt tears prick her eyelids.

"Righto, then, let's go!" Finch sounded more welcoming now. "It'll be sun-up in about half an hour." He looked at Audrey, and his expression changed. "Hey, is something wrong?"

"I'm okay. But – oh, Finch, Gummo died."

"Gummo?"

"One of my zebra finches. He couldn't fly properly any more. I found him dead yesterday afternoon. And the other finches didn't even *care*."

"They don't feel death like we do." Finch's voice was very gentle. "I'm real sorry about your bird. Let's see if we can take your mind off it."

The morning had lightened to a misty, pearly grey. Sniffing back her tears, thankful they hadn't fallen, Audrey peered at her watch: not even six-thirty yet.

She and Finch walked away from the cave, Snowy trotting at their heels. Soon the sandstone slabs and boulders along the line of the creek became smaller and more scattered, and trees grew more thickly. After about fifteen minutes they came to a waterhole surrounded by beds of rushes and sheltered by a giant weeping willow. The surface of the water was pale gold, reflecting the dawn sky.

"The water level's down a bit now," Finch said, "but it's not too bad for the end of summer. A spring keeps it topped up."

A bird took off from a partly submerged log underneath the willow and whirred away, leaving a trail of sparkling drops.

"Oh, look!" cried Audrey. "That was a sacred kingfisher! *Todiramphus sanctus*! Sorry if that sounds like I'm showing off," she added. "I don't know all the scientific names, only some of them. *Todiramphus* is on my bird poster."

"Yeah? I'm not much good at that sort of thing," Finch said. "Reckon I left school too early. The only name I know is kookaburra: *Dacelo* something?"

"It's *Dacelo novaeguineae*. That's on my bird poster too."

"I'll try to remember it." He was silent for a moment. "So what do you think of this place?"

"It's beautiful. Magic."

"I reckon it's the best place in the world. You never know what you'll see. There's a heron's nest a bit further along, and once I saw a boobook owl in that tree over there. Great big eyes staring at me."

Audrey crouched and dabbled her fingers in the water. It was icy cold. "What's your favourite bird, Finch?"

"Don't think I have one. Do you?"

"I don't know. Lots, really. Wrens are so pretty, and so are parrots – oh, and of course owls. I've been collecting owl ornaments for ages. And I love galahs, the way they waddle around like fat old ladies." She stood up and dried her hands on her T-shirt. "I saw a whistling kite a few weeks ago. It was so cool. Sometimes I try to imagine what it would be like to be a kite or a hawk, hovering way up in the sky, looking down on everything. I wish I could fly. It would be so amazing."

"I've always wanted to fly, too," said Finch. "If I could choose to be any sort of bird I wanted, I reckon I'd be a peregrine falcon. There's something extra special about falcons. They're right at the top of the pecking order, and they know it."

"*Falco peregrinus*," Audrey said under her breath. She could see the bird clearly in her mind's eye: its small, proud black head, its powerful hooked beak, its elegant shadow-striped feathers and the softness of its creamy bib. "I went to a falconry centre last year," she told Finch. "They did hunting displays there with different raptors – falcons and kestrels and eagles. Mum and Dad took me there for a birthday present. It was exciting, but it was still kind of sad because the birds weren't wild, they were having to entertain people, and I wondered if all the time they just really wanted to be free. The peregrines had to wear these little hoods, so they couldn't see. It's supposed to keep them calm until their handler needs them to hunt."

"Their eyesight is ten times as strong as ours," Finch said. "And did you know that when a falcon stoops, when it dives to catch its prey, it's travelling at around two hundred miles an hour? I read that in *Ripley's Believe It Or Not*." He shook his head. "That's definitely the sort of bird I'd want to be. But since I can't be a falcon, the next best thing would be to fly a plane. I've got this dream that one day I'll get my pilot's licence. I'd take Snowy up with me, give him a little pair of flying goggles. What d'you reckon?"

"That'd be so awesome. And I'd love to see Snowy in goggles." How was it possible, Audrey thought, that she could be so comfortable, so easy, with someone she'd only just met? She felt closer to Finch than she'd ever felt to anyone else in her whole life – anyone outside the family, at least. It made her dizzy with happiness and wonder. "Do you think you really might fly a plane one day?"

"I'd like to. Hey, then we could go flying

together," said Finch. "That'd be good, wouldn't it? You, me and Snowy." He beckoned to her. "I said I didn't have a favourite bird, but actually I do. I've got something to show you."

A little further on was a stretch of flat marshy land covered in low tea-tree, thickly matted ferns and dense, tough sedges. The distant line of the sea was silver now; the sun, almost peeking over the hills, cast long shadows.

The light spatter of birdsong became a chorus: first the carol of magpies, then the squeaky twittering of a host of smaller birds, rising and falling, growing louder as the sunlight grew brighter.

"Sit, Snowy," Finch ordered. He turned to Audrey. "Hold still. We might have to wait a bit."

After about five minutes, something started to come out from a clump of fern in front of them. A rabbit? A mouse? No, a bird. A tiny brownish bird.

Audrey held her breath.

Two more tiny birds came skittering up out of the bush. They trilled and chirruped in soft voices, flitting around, darting at insects, entirely absorbed in their early-morning ritual. Round tawny bodies streaked with black. Two with a blue-grey breast and throat, one without. Two males and a female, then. All had the same distinctive tail: six long, dark, wispy feathers.

Audrey stared at them, drinking in the sight as if it were some miraculous apparition that might disappear at any second. "Wow," she whispered. "I can't believe it. This is so brilliant."

"Pretty little things, aren't they?" Finch whispered back. "D'you know what they are?"

"Southern emu-wrens." Audrey glanced at him. "This must be one of the last colonies here. They're rare birds, endangered."

"I don't think they're that rare. There's quite a few of them around if you know where to look. These three come out most mornings, but they don't go far. I reckon they're happy being right here."

"Mavis says they've almost disappeared from this area. All the development is destroying their habitat. Farming and vineyards, stuff like that."

"Who's Mavis?"

"Oh, she's just this old lady who lives down the road from us. She's into birdwatching." She looked back at the wrens, still flitting about. "Mavis would love to see these little guys."

But Finch was gazing beyond her. "Sun's almost properly up," he said. "Time for me to go, I reckon."

"Do you have to?" Audrey asked. "It's still so early. Can't we stay for a bit longer?"

"Come round to the cave again. I'll be there, I promise."

In the first blinding rays of sunshine he was just a dark shape. Audrey couldn't see his face.

"Wait," she said. "Wait a few seconds. Please."

She turned away from him, hoping for one more glimpse of the emu-wrens. To her sorrow the little birds had disappeared. Very quietly, holding her breath, she moved closer to the patch of ferns, still searching, still hoping, but there was no longer any sign of life.

When she turned back, Finch and Snowy had gone.

Bewildered, Audrey stared. Nothing, not a trace of the boy or the dog. The light dazzled her eyes.

"Finch!" she called. "Finch, where are you? Wait for me! *Finch!*"

Audrey followed the creek all the way back to the

cave, and still there was no sign of him. She was puzzled, and disappointed. Why had he left so quickly? Of course he had to be careful to keep out of sight, but … They hadn't even said goodbye to each other, not properly.

She walked slowly back up the hill, her long spidery shadow walking beside her. The eastern sky was fleecy with drifts of tiny pink clouds like feathers, like the breast feathers of a galah.

If only she had a phone! She imagined herself posting a selfie on Instagram. *Me and Finch and some COOOOL birds*, she said in her mind. *Heart emoji, smiley face emoji.* That would make them all think!

She couldn't wait to tell Mavis about the emu-wrens. Then she realised that she couldn't tell anybody – for a start, she couldn't let on about Finch, and then there was the question of trespassing on Frank Blix's land – and her happiness subsided a little.

The back door was still unlocked. She opened it, tiptoed into the house and closed it carefully. Freddy bounded up to greet her, and pawed at the shut door.

"You want to go out, Fred? I guess it's late enough for you not to get into trouble. There you go." She let Freddy out and then crept down the hallway to her bedroom, sinking down at last on to her soft, comfortable bed.

In seconds she was asleep.

CHAPTER 13

Chloe came home on Sunday evening, her fingernails painted glittery purple. "It's called 'Sultry Plum'," she said, waving her fingers in Audrey's face. She'd had the most excellent time. *Goosebumps* was scary, and they'd also watched *Ghost Squad*, which had totally creeped her out. Emma had a TV in her bedroom, a Pandora bracelet with six charms on it and her very own iPhone. ("I know what you're going to say," Dad interrupted. "And you can forget it, right now.") Emma's parents were cool, too – they'd given Chloe a box of little pastries with chocolate in them to take home.

"They look a bit stale," said Mum in an undertone to Dad, and then, in a louder voice, "That was very kind of them, Chloe. I hope you thanked them for having you to stay."

"What d'you think? Of course I did."

"Maybe Emma would like to come round and help us pick grapes this week," said Dad.

Chloe looked at him in horror. "I don't think so."

"Well, there's no reason why you and Audrey can't give us a hand."

Mum frowned at him. "Ian, I've already told you, there's no way I'm allowing them to take time off school. You can use paid pickers like everyone else."

"Calm down, Caroline," said Dad. "Of course I'm going to use paid pickers. I just thought the kids would like to join in at some point, when they aren't at school. They might even enjoy the experience."

"It could be fun, Mum," said Audrey. "I don't mind. Really."

Dad tried again. "Caroline, grape pickers cost a good deal of money. The going rate is more than twenty bucks an hour. Families should pull together at times like these. I'd like to feel I have your total support."

"We didn't get much support from you when you were taking care of business, as you so brilliantly put it."

"You've no right to drag that up again—"

"If you hadn't—"

Audrey and Chloe walked quietly out of the room.

"Mum and Dad still aren't talking," said Chloe as they got ready for school on Monday morning.

"How d'you know that?"

"Mum said three words to him this morning. 'No', and 'Get stuffed'."

"You shouldn't listen to people's conversations."

"I wasn't exactly *listening*. I *heard*. And it wasn't exactly a *conversation*."

Audrey struggled into her backpack. It seemed even heavier than usual this morning. "I hate it when they fight."

"You can't totally blame Mum, can you?" Chloe said, dabbing on some lip gloss from a little pot. She held it out. "See what Emma gave me? Smell – it's like strawberries. Mum never wanted to live out here. It was Dad's fault, not hers."

"Dad lost his job," Audrey reminded her. Chloe was so irritating when she talked in that knowing, grown-up way. "He had to do something. What was he going to do, be on hand-outs for the rest of his life?"

"Why couldn't he just find another job?"

"How should I know? Why don't you ask him?"

"Why don't *you*?"

Mum came into the kitchen. "Get a move on, you two. It's nearly a quarter to nine. You're going to be late for school."

"You haven't given us our lunch yet," Chloe said.

"Oh, for goodness sake." Mum grabbed her purse, pulled out two ten-dollar notes, and gave them one each. "There you are. Buy yourselves something fatty and disgusting from the canteen. Keep the change."

Audrey and Chloe looked at each other. This wasn't the Mum they knew: the Mum who insisted they always have a proper lunch of wholemeal bread sandwiches and vegetable sticks and at least one piece of fruit.

"Thanks, Mum."

"Thanks, Mum."

"Cool," Chloe said to Audrey. "I'm getting sausage rolls and a strawberry milk."

"Righto, Mum, we're ready," said Audrey. "Bye, Freddy. Be a good boy."

"See ya, Fred." Chloe stopped to stroke him, and he turned over on his back and purred. She bent down to rub his furry belly.

"Chloe, do hurry up," called Mum. She rushed for the back door, car keys in her hand. Then she stopped. "Audrey, did I hear you say 'righto'? Where on earth did that come from? My grandfather used to say that."

"The grapes are ready to pick," Dad announced when they were having dinner on Tuesday night. "Since I can't use you kids during school hours, I suppose I'll have to get some pickers organised. I'd like to get things moving by Thursday at the latest. A good team of pickers should clear up five hectares in a day or so, shouldn't they?"

"I've absolutely no idea," said Mum. "I suppose it

depends how experienced they are."

"I'll get on the phone after dinner and see who can start when," said Dad. "Mavis has given me some phone numbers to ring, local people who might be available. She's even offered to help us herself, believe it or not. "

"Really? She looks far too old for that sort of work."

"Don't you believe it. She's probably nothing like as ancient as she looks. Women like her look old before their time, but they're as tough as old boots."

"That reminds me," said Mum. "When I was in town today I popped into the bakery to get some rolls for school lunches, and Janice, the woman who served me, said that Mavis's brother died on the weekend. Remember, Mavis mentioned that he'd been ill? He was quite a local character, Janice said. His funeral's this Friday."

Dad sighed. "Oh lord. Should we pay our respects?"

"We certainly should do something. I'll see if I can find a card, something appropriate. Poor Mavis. I wonder if she was very close to her brother."

"Who knows?" said Dad. "From what I've heard,

it sounds as if he was more of a burden. She spent a lot of time looking after him, helping him out."

"Poor old Mavis."

After they'd had dessert, Dad rose from the table, picked up a list of phone numbers and his mobile, and went into the living room.

Audrey piled up the dirty dishes. "It's your turn to wash, Mum."

"Really? It always seems to be my turn. Very well, you can dry."

When they were halfway through the washing up Dad came back into the kitchen, looking annoyed.

"I can't round up anyone till Friday, would you believe! Of course all the crops are ready to pick right now, and these people go to the bigger places where the money is, or where they've had a contract for years. Nobody really wants to be bothered with a piddling little vineyard like ours. It's like they're doing you a favour."

"Oh, Ian." Mum put down the dishcloth. "Who can you get on Friday?"

"There's a husband-and-wife team, the Longmores, and a local woman, Doris Schultz. They've all said they can come to us when they've finished at Bill Brewer's next door. And Doris is going to see if her niece can help too. So that's a potential team of four. Three of them pretty much certain, one possible. And me, of course."

It's a pity Finch can't help, thought Audrey. *He could do with the money.* She imagined introducing him to Mum and Dad. *Mum, Dad, this is Finch. He's my friend. I met him in a cave.* It was too bad she'd promised she wouldn't tell anyone about him. And of course there was the problem of Bill Brewer as well. She couldn't remember Finch saying his uncle had vines.

"What size vineyard has Bill Brewer got, Dad?" she asked.

"I'm not too sure. Maybe twenty hectares? He harvests most of his crop by machine, but he has a few hectares of premium grapes that have to be picked by hand. In a few years' time, I hope we'll be near that level too."

"Have you ever met him?"

"I went round to see him the other day, actually. Introduced myself, had a chat."

"Did he show you his pigs?"

"What is this, Twenty Questions? I didn't know

he had any pigs. Who told you that?"

Oops. "Oh, just someone at school."

"I've no idea. If he does have pigs, I don't know where he'd put them."

Audrey decided to drop the subject of the pigs. She picked up a bowl and dried it carefully. "Mavis said he had a dog."

"Yeah, one of those big black monsters. He seems to be a pleasant sort of chap, though. Middle-aged. Has a nice wife."

And this pleasant sort of chap is a bully who uses kids for slave labour. But she couldn't say that, of course. She took a dripping dinner plate from Mum and wiped the soapsuds off it. "So how do you think we'll go with our crop, Dad?"

"Fingers crossed," Dad put his arm around Audrey's shoulders, "our crop is looking pretty good. Better than I expected, in fact. Really not bad at all."

Friday morning dawned hot and sultry. A strange yellowish light made the vines look greener than ever. Two large rectangular metal bins had been set up beside the vineyard, ready to take the crop.

It turned out that Doris Schultz's niece couldn't come because she had to make an emergency visit to the dentist. But Doris herself, and Kylie and Darryl Longmore, turned up at the vineyard on the dot of seven o'clock. Doris, a tiny energetic woman in a grey tracksuit and a cotton bonnet, was clearly the most experienced picker in this little group. She sized up her patch, grabbed a couple of plastic buckets and started work immediately.

Chloe and Audrey stood watching, and Dad hovered around Doris, not sure what to do, yet trying to look as if he was in charge.

"You can be the bucket boy," Doris said to him helpfully. "Empty out the full ones into the big bin, and bring back the empties. That way we don't have to keep lugging buckets all over the place. It's like an assembly line, y'know?"

"Sounds like a good idea," said Dad. "Ah – it's actually my first harvest. I'm going to be a bit slow to start with, until I get the hang of it."

Doris stood back, a bunch of grapes in one hand, a pair of secateurs in the other, and looked him up and down. "Don't worry, it's not that hard. And you're a big strong boy, so you'll do fine. Maybe you can get a few grapes picked as well. Just don't let us pickers down. We don't want to be scouting around for an empty bucket while you're off somewhere else."

"Isn't it funny to hear someone talking to Dad like that?" Chloe whispered to Audrey. "It's like he's a little kid."

"To Doris he probably *is* a little kid," Audrey whispered back. "She would've been picking grapes before he was born."

Chloe giggled. "I wish we could stay and watch."

But now Mum was running up, waving at them and yelling, "Audrey! Chloe! Come on you two, get a move on!" And in the usual chaos of eating breakfast, finding homework, packing bags and working out the day's program, the harvest was soon forgotten.

CHAPTER 14

When Chloe and Audrey came home from school, later than usual because Chloe had tennis practice, the grape pickers were still toiling away.

Dad came over to meet the car as Mum pulled up in the driveway. His face and arms looked sunburned. When he took off his hat, he revealed a line of dirt and sweat on his forehead.

"Nice hat hair, Dad," laughed Chloe, patting his head with her tennis racquet.

"Thanks for noticing, Princess," said Dad. He turned to Mum. "Doris and the others are knocking off in a few minutes, and we've still got about a quarter of the vineyard to be picked."

"I'd say you've done well," remarked Mum. "Are the bins full?"

"One is. The other's about a third full, I guess."

"Can't you ask the pickers to stay on and finish the job?"

"I don't think so. They've been going for nearly ten hours straight, with only half an hour off for lunch. That Doris is amazing – she picks two buckets to Kylie's one, and about six to each one of mine. I've never felt so useless in my life. But we've all reached our limit, and even Doris is ready to go home now. Trouble is, no one can come in to pick tomorrow – they've all got other things lined up – and according to the weather forecast there's a storm brewing."

"Does that matter? You'll just need to cover the bins so the rain doesn't get in."

Dad took out a handkerchief and wiped his forehead. "It could be a lot worse than that. They say there's going to be a massive hailstorm. Hail could strip the bunches, and at the very least there'd be split skins and other damage." He stuffed his handkerchief back in his pocket. "Then again, the storm could simply blow away. We'll see how things shape up tomorrow."

After Dad had paid off the pickers, he came in for a late cup of tea. "Phwoar!" he said. "That's the most strenuous thing I've done in a while. Could've done with you kids to carry the buckets – I was racing around like a blue-arsed fly trying to keep up with everyone and get my own rows picked." He looked hopefully at Audrey and Chloe. "D'you think you two might give me a hand tomorrow? I'm going to get on with the picking on my own. It's too big a risk to leave everything till Monday."

Chloe looked at Audrey. "Sure, I guess."

Audrey looked at Mum. "Okay with you, Mum?"

"I suppose so. I didn't want you skipping school, that's all. What you do on Saturday is your own business."

By the time Saturday morning dawned, everyone was feeling anxious and unsettled. Dad had gone out to start picking as soon as it was light. Audrey could see him from the kitchen window, his head in its straw hat bobbing along the rows.

When she went outside to feed her finches, she realised that the heat and humidity were even worse than they'd been yesterday. The finches were cheeping quietly, sitting high on their perches in the deep shade of the roof. There was no other sound, and the silence was eerie. The sky was blue, but grey-and-white clouds were boiling up menacingly on the horizon.

She went back inside. Chloe was lying on the sofa in the living room, watching cartoons on television. Audrey walked up to the TV and switched it off.

Chloe sat up indignantly. "I was watching that!"

"Come on, Chlo. Dad's all on his own out there."

"It's too hot!" moaned Chloe. But she slid off the sofa immediately. "Let's go."

"Hats," said Mum, walking past with an armful of clothes to be washed. "And sunscreen."

Chloe ran to her bedroom for her orange Sportsgirl beach hat, and when Audrey got the big bottle of SPF50 from the bathroom cupboard, she cheerfully rubbed the white lotion on her face and arms and legs. "It's like going to the beach," she said, giving the bottle back to Audrey. "I wish we *were* going to the beach."

Audrey put sunscreen on her nose. "This'll be heaps more fun."

In fact, as Chloe reminded Audrey afterwards, it wasn't fun at all, but hard work. The vineyard wasn't large, but when you were standing at the beginning of the rows of vines, they seemed to go on forever.

Dad organised Chloe to do the bucket run, and Audrey to pick. They were picking on the far side of the vineyard, and it was a long walk to the bins, so emptying the filled buckets and replacing them with empties was a full-time job.

"Right, Audrey," said Dad, "this section of three rows can be your patch. I've nearly finished my rows, and then I'll start on the three above you. I reckon that works best, rather than us doing row by row. Suit you?"

Audrey nodded. "Sure." She pulled on a pair of too-big gardening gloves and started on her first row. The grapes hung heavily, fat, purple-bloomed, already warm from the sun – dozens of them on each vine. Mostly they were easy to see; sometimes they were partly hidden beneath the leaves. *Snip, snip, snip.* One by one the bunches plopped into the bucket. Within a few minutes it was full, and Audrey grabbed the next empty bucket in the line. *Snip, snip, snip.* The secateur blades flashed.

"Ouch!" There was a cut in the finger of Audrey's left glove, and blood was already seeping into the fabric. She pulled off the glove to inspect her wound. *"Dad!"*

Dad rounded the end of the row and ran up to her. "Did you hurt yourself? Those secateurs are razor-sharp." He dug in his pocket for a box of bandaids, and stuck one on Audrey's damaged finger. "Not that I should talk. I've cut myself three times so far." He hugged her, quickly. "Be more careful, now, won't you?"

Surprisingly, the finger didn't really hurt, although the cut was quite deep. Audrey started to pick again, beginning at the top of the vine and then working her way down. Each plant was trellised on two wires. The grapes on the lower trellis wire hung almost down to the ground, and before long Audrey found that her back was beginning to ache. Sweat ran down her face and into her eyes, and annoying little flies floated around her head and settled on her nose and lips. Reddish juice mingled with the blood on her left glove. There was a heady, winy smell of ripe grapes.

Chloe raced up and down the rows, carrying the full buckets away and hurling empties back down the line. Beneath her hat her face was scarlet.

It took Audrey nearly an hour to finish her first row. Two more to go, and that was just for starters. She'd pulled off the gloves – they were so big that she worked more quickly without them – and inside its now filthy bandaid her cut finger had started to throb. Dad had almost finished his three rows. He was picking an entire row in around forty minutes. It was a speed Audrey was sure she'd never reach.

"Time for a break," said Dad, when they'd been working for two hours. At the side of the vineyard, in the shade of a big gum tree, were the old tartan picnic rug and the esky. Dad spread the rug over the dry, prickly grass, and Audrey opened the esky and brought out three big bottles of iced water.

Chloe flung herself back on the rug. "Dad, I'm *dying*!"

Dad allowed them ten minutes. They drank their

water and looked out over the vineyard. Even the birds were silent today, and in the breathless air the plastic hawk scarers hung motionless in their places, scaring nothing.

"I don't want to do this," Audrey said to herself. "It's hot and sticky, and my back hurts, and my finger hurts, and my brain hurts." She thought of the house with its cooling fan, the appeal of non-strenuous activities like watching TV, reading a book, eating ice cream …

"I must say I don't like the look of that weather," Dad said.

The sky directly above them was still a brilliant blue, but to the west, over the sea, it was now grey. A deep, livid purple-grey.

Dad put the half-empty water bottles back in the esky. "That cold front's coming in fast," he said, "so who knows how much time we've got left. Let's get moving."

Audrey picked now without even thinking about what she was doing. She moved steadily down the row, trying to ignore her aching back and the pain of her cut finger.

"Can you speed things up a bit, Audrey?" yelled

Dad. "We're not going to make it unless we go faster than this. And where the hell's Chloe? I've run out of buckets."

Audrey straightened up. She could see her sister under the gum tree, probably getting another drink from the esky. "Chloe!" she shouted. "We need buckets!"

Chloe waved at her and came racing back, two empty buckets in each hand. "Sorry."

Audrey picked up a bucket and moved to the next vine. "We've got to work faster, Dad says. You haven't got time to do your own thing whenever you feel like it." She wiped sweat from her eyes. "We could really do with another pair of hands."

Chloe gave her a smug little look. "Well, you might just get them," she said.

"What? Are you going to pick *and* do the bucket run? Not likely. You can hardly keep up with us as it is. Oh, I know. You've asked Freddy."

"Just you wait," said Chloe.

CHAPTER 15

Snip, snip, snip. Snip, snip, snip. One by one, but so slowly, the buckets filled with dark purple grapes. Hordes of tiny brown grasshoppers leaped out of the dried grass below the vines with small clicking sounds. A sulphur-crested cockatoo screeched noisily from a gum tree. *Cacatua galerita.* The words lodged in Audrey's tired brain and repeated themselves, over and over. She started to pick to the rhythm: *Caca* – snip – *tua* – drop; *gale* – snip – *rita* – drop. Another bucket full. A breeze wafted over the vines. Audrey felt its coolness on her face.

A shout made her look up. Three people were

walking up the hill. Mavis. A man Audrey didn't recognise. And Mum. *Mum?* Chloe was running towards them. Audrey put her secateurs on a post, marking her spot, and followed. Dad was already there.

"You know I can't pick," said Mum. "But I can at least help Chloe pass out the buckets or something."

"Caroline, that's fantastic," said Dad. "Anything you do will be a huge help. Mavis! This is a surprise! And Bill – I thought you'd be flat out with your own vintage."

"Finished yesterday," said the man called Bill. "When I got the call from Mavis I reckoned you could do with a bit of help. These your kids? G'day, I'm Bill Brewer, got the place next to yours."

Audrey stared at him, open-mouthed. *Bill Brewer?* The whole image of the person she'd built up in her head fell to pieces and vanished. This man looked so ordinary! Dark, thinning hair. A typical farmer's face, tanned and weather-beaten, unshaven. Deep laughter crinkles around the eyes. The only unexpected thing about him was a small gold earring. Was this really the man who'd bullied Finch and sunk his boot into poor little Snowy's ribs?

Audrey realised that she was gawping. She closed her mouth. Then she opened it again. "Hi," she muttered.

Dad didn't notice Audrey's embarrassment. "Did you say you had a call from Mavis, Bill?"

"Yeah. I always do what Mavis tells me." He winked at Mavis. "After all, she *is* my aunty."

"Mavis is your *aunty*?" said Audrey. She was so shocked that for a moment it didn't register that she was actually speaking to Finch's Uncle Bill, pig man, kicker of dogs.

"Well, kind of. Don't ask me to figure it out right now, we've got work to do." He scanned the sky. "Looks nasty up there."

"Just point us in the right direction, Ian," said Mavis. "G'day Audrey, Chloe." She was wearing a green plastic apron covered with pictures of seahorses. It looked as if it had been cut from an old shower curtain. Her red baseball cap was pulled down firmly over her white hair. "Haven't picked for a while," she admitted, "but many hands make light work, eh?"

"You did this, didn't you?" Audrey said to Chloe as they all walked back up the hill to the vineyard.

There was a new feeling of lightness in the air, in spite of the threatening sky.

"Yeah, Dad left his mobile in the esky. I saw it when we got our drinks. I texted Mum and asked her if she could *please* help, we were desperate, and she said she'd phone Mavis, cause Mavis offered to give us a hand earlier, remember? And Mavis must've phoned Mr Brewer." She did a little skip, looking pleased with herself. "Good plan, hey? I'm glad I saw Dad's mobile. He never would've asked Mum. He would've just gone on trying to give himself a heart attack."

"Excellent plan, Chlo." Looking at her, Audrey wondered at her little sister. Chloe was always so confident, so sure of herself. She worked out what to do, and then she did it. Finch was the same. *They'd get on really well*, she thought. *I wonder if they'll ever meet? I wish Finch didn't have to be a secret. I'd like everyone to know about him.*

She started picking again, and found to her surprise that she didn't feel tired any more. It was amazing what a difference it made to know that she and Dad weren't struggling through the last twenty-odd rows all by themselves.

Mavis was already halfway down her row. Audrey watched her, trying to work out how Mavis could pick so quickly. She hardly seemed to bend and stretch at all, and she reached for the grape bunches as if she knew exactly where they'd be waiting for her.

Further up the vineyard Bill Brewer was also working steadily and swiftly. He and Mavis encouraged and teased each other, turning the picking into a friendly competition. *He doesn't seem to be such a bad guy*, Audrey thought. But no – Finch wouldn't have lied about him. She hardened her heart again. "Pig man," she said fiercely to herself. "I wish I could tell Dad, and then Dad could – I don't know – report him to the police or something. He shouldn't get away with what he's done." She checked the vine she'd just picked, found two bunches of grapes she'd missed, and groaned.

Half an hour later, distant thunder started to rumble. Lightning cracked and sizzled. Audrey turned at the strainer post that marked the end of her row and stood for a moment, easing her tired shoulders. After the next flash of lightning she started to count. There were only a few seconds between lightning and thunder – the storm was getting close. Not much time left. She counted the rows still to be picked. Four! Could they make it?

Another lightning flash, and then a deafening thunderclap. Dad straightened up like a jack-in-the-box and waved his arms. "We've got one row each, and then we're done. It's us against the weather. Let's go!"

This must be how a horse feels at the end of a race, thought Audrey. The ache in her back had returned, and she'd snipped another finger, this time taking off half a fingernail. Her arms were scratched from elbow to wrist. No longer able to bend, she now picked grapes from the lower wires on her knees, and her jeans were filthy with grape juice and dirt. She was more tired than she'd ever been in her life, but a huge feeling of excitement and anticipation was driving her on. "Nearly there," she told herself. "Only ten more vines. Nine ... Eight ... Seven ..."

Snip, snip, snip ...

Done!

"Buckets, Chlo!"

Chloe rushed up to her and together they struggled down to the big steel bins, each carrying two overflowing buckets. Mavis and Bill Brewer were carrying their last buckets down too, and Mum was already helping Dad with the tarpaulin bin covers. As Audrey reached up to empty the first of her buckets, lightning lit up the whole sky.

"Quick!" shouted Dad. "Chuck the grapes in, and let's get these tarps on!"

The sky held its breath for that moment. And then, slowly at first, and then faster, the rain came.

CHAPTER 16

"Run!" shouted Chloe. She was dancing with excitement, eyes shining, hair hanging around her face in wet tendrils. Dad snatched up the esky and the rug, and they all made a dash for the house. Mavis ripped off her shower-curtain apron and held it over Mum and herself as they jogged together down the hill.

Moments later they were all in the kitchen, laughing and talking, amazed that they'd beaten the weather. Mum made tea and piled currant buns and shortbread fingers on plates, and everyone ate hungrily. Dad flung open the window to let in some cooler air. The smell of wet earth and soaked dry grass filled the room. Mum turned on the jug again to make more tea.

Then, "Rain's stopped," said Audrey.

Everyone stopped talking and listened, waiting, heads cocked, like birds. In the silence outside, the sound of the electric jug was very loud. The sun shone brightly, but in seconds the kitchen was dark again.

The first crack on the tin roof was like a hurled stone, the impact shocking in the silence. Then came another. *Crack*. Then another, and another, faster. *Crack-crack-crack*. The hurled stones became machine-gun fire.

Audrey raced to the window. "It's hailing golf balls!" she shouted. "Look!"

In the backyard, hailstones were bouncing on brick paving, ripping through tree branches, shredding leaves, smashing plants into the ground. A small white form bolted across the open space, ears back, body low to the ground, dodging and weaving to avoid the ricocheting balls of ice.

"Freddy!" called Chloe. She ran to the back door and held it open.

The cat was drenched, his flattened wet fur revealing his surprisingly thin body and rabbity head. He streaked into the kitchen, settled down beneath the table and started to lick himself dry.

Standing outside, sheltering under the back verandah, Audrey watched, open-mouthed, while everything was enveloped by an explosion of noise. Chloe came out to join her. "Isn't it awesome?" she said. But the storm was as brief as it was fierce, and in less than a minute it was gone, leaving behind heaped drifts of ice. Steam rose as wetness evaporated from the warm paving bricks.

"Wow," said Audrey. "Lucky we got the grapes in. Imagine what the vines look like now."

A metal watering can that had been left outside was tipped onto its side, a buckled mess. The cover of the rainwater tank was pocked with marks like bullet holes. Hailstones had pelted the finch cage, leaving a long crack in the wooden roof. Inside, on the top perch, the four remaining Marx Brothers huddled close together, their pecking order forgotten.

The back door creaked and banged as the others came outside to look.

"Never seen anything like that," said Bill Brewer.

"Thank the lord I got my crop in, is all I can say. I'd better get on home to check the damage."

"Me too," said Mavis. "My Daphne's probably having kittens. Last time we had a storm she ended up under the quilt on my bed, poor old girl, and when she's scared she wets herself, unfortunately. It's rough on animals, isn't it? They can't understand what's going on. Mind you," she added, "weather like we've had today isn't natural. Make no mistake, it's because the world's warming up. People who don't think climate change is happening are kidding themselves."

There was a murmur of agreement, and then Mum and Dad shook hands with Bill Brewer, and both of them hugged Mavis. "Thanks," said Dad. "We'd never have got the crop in on our own. Mavis, you must have had a lot on your mind recently, with your brother passing away, and we appreciate your help all the more. If Caroline and I can repay the favour–"

Mavis waved his words away. "Happy to do it," she said. "It's what neighbours are for. Come on, Bill. Let's see what little surprises Mother Nature has left for us."

During the night, Audrey woke to hear rain hammering down on the roof, a steady downpour. *It sounds so good*, she thought sleepily. Rain wasn't exciting and destructive like hail. It was friendly and comforting, and promised good things: an overflowing rainwater tank, green grass, growth and freshness. The creek would run strongly again, and the waterhole would be properly full. Finch would like that.

The storm had finally driven away the sultry stuffiness, and the air was deliciously cool. Audrey pulled her quilt up around her ears. Her muscles ached pleasantly. Snug in her bed, listening to the drumming of the raindrops, she fell asleep again. And the rain kept falling.

CHAPTER 17

Audrey had barely crawled out of bed late on Sunday morning when Dad came stomping into the kitchen, his shirt soaked, his boots making dirty wet marks on the floor tiles. The rain had settled to a fine drizzle: outside the window everything looked misty. The glory vine on the back verandah was hung with raindrops.

"Ian, boots off, please!" Mum was fussing around like a wet hen. "I washed this floor only two days ago! Look at the mud you're bringing in!"

"Bad Dad," Chloe said cheekily, looking up from her bowl of toasted muesli.

Dad snorted, but he kicked his boots off and slung them out through the back door. "Well, it's all over," he said. "The guys from the winery have come and picked up our bins, and that's that. Next time we see those grapes they'll be in a bottle of some very fine wine."

"Oh, that *is* good news," said Mum. "All the hard work rewarded. We hope. Did you settle on a final price with the winery?"

"Yes, and not too bad either. Enough to tide us over, at least." He cut a thick slice of bread and put it in the toaster, holding his hands over the top to warm them. "You won't believe how cold it is outside now. The temperature has dropped around fifteen degrees, just like that. One of the winery guys reckons the creek broke its banks last night and the ford down the road's flowing at a couple of metres. We should go down to have a look later."

Mum went over to the kitchen bench to make coffee. "How much rain did we have? It didn't sound as if it let up all night."

"It didn't. We've had over seventy millimetres – a massive amount for this time of year."

"Nice for the garden," Mum said. "Although

it'll take a while to recover from the storm damage, I suppose. I haven't been out yet to see how bad that is."

Audrey still felt sleep-fuddled. She poured herself a glass of orange juice, and watched as the condensation trickled slowly down the side of the glass.

"Did you say something about the creek, Dad?"

"Yeah. The bin guy says it's flooded. Running a banker, he said."

"Wow. Can we go see?"

"Sure. Right after breakfast."

"Cool."

Wearing raincoats and last winter's rubber boots, they set off for the ford. Tiny streams flowed down the road embankments, and tree branches, their leaves heavy with water, hung low. Both sides of the dirt road were crumbly with gravel washouts, and its pounded surface was slick and slippery.

"Watch out!" called Dad as Chloe skidded a couple of steps and only saved herself from falling by clutching his sleeve.

"Watch out yourself," Chloe yelled back. She grabbed a low-hanging branch and shook it, showering Dad with drops. Dad pulled back the branch and ripped off handfuls of leaves, stuffing them down the back of Chloe's coat. She squealed, ran and slid into Mum.

"Really, Ian, how old do you think you are?" said Mum, but her voice wasn't angry. Then they were all showering each other with dripping branches, throwing handfuls of leaves and wet grass, and laughing themselves silly.

Mum took Dad's arm. Audrey took Mum's other arm, and Chloe took hers, and they all walked down the road together.

Audrey leaned into her mother. "Happy, Mum?" she asked.

"Happi*er*," Mum said. And then she smiled and said, "*Much* happier."

They passed Mavis's house, all its garden ornaments washed by rain and shining in the weak sunlight. From behind the house came a distant clucking as a hen announced a newly laid egg.

Big puddles stretched across Mavis's front garden,

and the birdbath with its patient fishing gnome was full to the brim.

Audrey pointed at him. "You think he might catch something now, Chlo?"

"I hope so. I kinda like that little guy."

They could hear the water before they saw it: a low rushing, gurgling sound. Then they rounded the bend.

Mavis and Daphne were already at the ford. Daphne wore a tartan dog coat, and Mavis was wearing an ancient Driza-Bone, her hair hidden beneath a plastic hood.

Mavis grinned toothlessly at them. "Morning, all. This isn't something you see every day, is it?"

The ford had turned into a muddy lake that reached high up the road on either side. At its centre was a powerful surge of rapidly flowing water, eddying grass and sticks and caramel-coloured froth. Occasionally a bit of wood or rubbish floated past, and as they watched, a large torn-off gum-tree branch made its majestic way downstream, turning slowly in the current.

Everyone exclaimed at the quantity of water.

Audrey: "Wow!"

Chloe, with a delighted shudder: "Awesome!"

Mum: "Who would think this could happen to our little creek?"

Dad: "It's certainly been one hell of a downpour."

Mavis, looking serious: "The creek'll be busting its banks everywhere. It's a proper big flood this time."

Wait – didn't Mr Scardino say something about caves flooding? Audrey felt a prickle of fear. She turned to Mavis. "Is the whole creek like this?"

"Oh, for sure." Mavis's voice was rather muffled without her teeth. "I've seen it happen before. You get a real heavy rain like this and the creek bed can't handle it, and then bingo – you've got a flash flood."

"But the creek doesn't stay flooded. The water all drains into the sea, doesn't it?"

"That's right. It'll be gone in a day or so. You wouldn't want to be living too near the creek right now, though." She bent down and gave Daphne a slap on her flank. "Up you get, old girl. This dampness won't be doing your arthritis any good."

Daphne heaved herself up, gave herself a good shake and looked trustingly up at her owner.

Audrey couldn't speak. If the whole creek was

up, it must have flooded the cave. And if it had – what had happened to Finch?

"I'm going home," she said. "I need to check something." She began to jog back up the road, slipping and sliding in the mud, trying not to panic.

Soon there were splashy footsteps behind her. "Aud, what's up? Something's wrong, isn't it?"

Audrey slowed down. Should she tell Chloe? This might be an emergency, and if it was, then people would have to know about Finch. On the other hand, if he was all right, and she told people about him, then she would have betrayed him. But, oh, surely Chloe could keep a secret. Finch would understand, wouldn't he? … If he was still alive. Oh God. She had to tell Chloe. She simply had to.

"You know that cave I thought I saw down the creek? By the crooked tree? I've been there, sorry, I couldn't tell you, I promised, and someone's living in it. They could be in danger from the flood–"

"Don't walk so fast, Aud! What are you talking about? *Who's* living there?"

"A friend of mine. Remember the fox terrier that came round to our place? It belongs to him."

"*What*? You've got a *friend*? A *boyfriend*?

What's his name?"

"Finch. And he's not a boyfriend."

"Finch?"

Audrey waved her arms in irritation. "Stop repeating everything I say! It doesn't matter what his name is. The thing is, he could be in danger. We've got to get to the cave, *quickly!*"

CHAPTER 18

They had to go back to the farm to reach the creek where it curved through their property. The long wet grass lashed their legs as they ran.

"Why didn't you tell me about this?" panted Chloe. "I can't believe you didn't tell me."

"I promised Finch I wouldn't," said Audrey, between breaths. "It might have got him into trouble."

"What sort of trouble?"

"I can't say."

Chloe plunged after her. "What if he's – I mean, what if the flood–"

"We just have to check it out." Audrey flung the words over her shoulder. "The cave's probably well above water-level. It's quite a bit higher than the creek bed, isn't it?"

"Is it? I can't remember. Aud, slow down! He'll be okay, don't stress."

"Oh, Chlo, I hope you're right."

Chloe stumbled, almost falling. "Don't go so *fast*! I can't keep up. And my boots are eating my socks."

"Forget your stupid boots. Come *on*!"

The creek bed had disappeared beneath a surging torrent the colour of milky tea. They raced along the bank until they reached the boundary fence. Here they pulled up, breathing hard.

The distant crooked tree that grew above the cave was the only landmark Audrey recognised. Beneath it there was a swirling mass of water.

Audrey felt as if she'd been punched in the stomach. This was worse, far worse, than she'd expected.

Chloe grabbed her hand. "Aud, what – what if that boy is still, you know, in there?"

Audrey squeezed her little sister's cold fingers.

Her mouth felt stiff, as if it didn't belong to her, and it was shaping words in a language it didn't understand. "He won't be. He'll be all right. He'll have got out."

"But what if he *didn't*?" Chloe's eyes were huge. "What if he *drowned*?"

Drowned? Of course it was possible. He could have been asleep when the flood hit. He could have been taken by surprise. He could have been caught in the narrow entrance, pushed back by the force of the water ... *No.* Audrey shook the thoughts away. *No, no, not Finch. He's way too smart. He'll have got out of the cave, for sure. But if he did, where would he go? Where would he be now?* She looked across the flooded creek at the rain-soaked countryside beyond. She prayed that she'd catch a glimpse of Snowy, or that Finch's lanky figure would suddenly appear from somewhere. There was nothing. Just the grey sky and the roar and tumble of rushing water.

Her mind raced. Perhaps Finch had climbed the crooked tree and was hiding among its leaves. No, that was ridiculous – you'd see him a mile off. Perhaps he was sheltering behind that low outcrop of rocks. Perhaps he was on the road somewhere.

Perhaps.

Or perhaps he was still in the cave. Trapped.

No!

Audrey knew there was no point guessing what had happened.

"Chlo," she said, "we have to tell Mum and Dad."

"I know," said Chloe. "You wouldn't really be breaking your promise, would you? This is life and death. That's different."

"It is, isn't it?"

Chloe sniffed. "My nose is drippy. Got a tissue?"

Audrey burrowed in her pocket and produced a balled-up wad of Kleenex. Chloe blew her nose.

They were still holding hands as they made their way back up the hill.

Dad's face was grim. "Audrey, are you serious? There's a cave somewhere under all that water, and there could be a boy in there?"

"I didn't say he *was* in there. I said he *might* be."

"How do you know about this boy? Is he someone from school?"

Audrey was starting to feel desperate. It was like living through the sort of nightmare where everything moves in slow motion. Why were they wasting so much time, when Finch might be trapped and needing help? *You know that if he's still in the cave, he's past help*, said a voice in her brain. Audrey pushed the voice away. "His name's Finch. I came across him sort of by accident a while ago."

"But why is he in the cave, for heaven's sake?"

"It's complicated, Dad. I promised I wouldn't tell anyone about him. He has ... reasons for not living with his folks."

"How old is this boy?"

"I'm not sure. He's left school."

"*He's left school?*" Dad repeated, disbelief all over his face. "What were you – I mean, how–?"

"*Dad*! I didn't do anything wrong!"

"Of course you didn't, sweetheart. I'm sorry." Dad shook his head. "If he's that old, I'd say he would've had the good sense to get out. But we can't risk it. I'd better ring the SES. They're trained to cope with this sort of thing. They'll know what to do."

"This is a job for the police divers," said the State Emergency Service volunteer. "There's no other way we can get into that cave while the creek's this high."

They were all standing with the SES man on the slope that led down to the part of the creek where the cave was, Dad, Mum, Audrey and Chloe, shading their eyes against the sun that now shone brightly through the clouds. The torrent that surged down the creek bed gleamed with sky colours and earth colours. Was the water level falling? Audrey couldn't be sure.

She stared at the man's hi-vis orange jacket and tried to speak normally. "Do you think they'll find him?"

The man smiled wearily. "Look, chances are the kid got out in good time, as soon as the cave started to fill with water. That's what anyone with half a brain would do. But it's possible the cave hasn't filled completely. It could be there's a safe ledge inside it and your friend is still in there. But we don't know the score, we've got no idea. I'll get on to the police ASAP."

He looked Audrey right in the eyes, his face grey with tiredness. His expression, patient and concerned, made her feel guilty, as if she'd been caught out playing a thoughtless joke. Perhaps this man thought she was lying, a troublemaker.

Then she thought of Finch – maybe trapped, scared. "All I know is he *could* be in there. He's been living in the cave for a few weeks."

The SES man nodded, and pulled out his mobile. "Dee? Brad from the SES. Can you get me Vince? Ta."

He turned to Dad, and his voice took on a more confidential tone. "The kid's probably on the run. There's been a few vandals in the area lately, kids thieving, setting fire to property, that kind of thing. Chances are he'll turn up safe and sound before too long." He put the phone to his ear again. "That you, Vince? We've got a bit of a problem."

CHAPTER 19

They were all in the living room after late lunch: tomato soup and toasted cheese sandwiches – Audrey's favourite, but today the cheese tasted like cotton wool. Everybody had tried to find something to do while they waited for news. Dad and Chloe were slumped on the sofa watching cartoons on television, and Mum was sitting at the table mending Chloe's school uniform where the hem had come down. Audrey couldn't settle. She'd seen the cartoons before, she'd run out of books to read and she couldn't stop worrying about Finch. She flopped onto a chair next to Mum.

"When d'you think we'll hear from the police?"

"As soon as they've managed to get into the cave, I suppose."

"I just hope Finch is okay. Do you think he's okay?"

Mum put down her sewing. "Darling, I'm sure he'll be all right. I'm sure because from what you've told Dad and me, this boy is country-wise and extremely resourceful. He's also a local, isn't he? And he's not a baby – he's a teenager, and that means he has a bit of common sense. At least, we hope he has." She smiled wryly. "He's not the kind of person who's likely to get caught in a flooded cave. He would have been aware of the danger and he would have got out long before it became a problem."

"What if he *couldn't* get out? What if something awful's happened to him?"

"Probably nothing has." Mum's face was full of pity and concern. "He's your friend, isn't he? You care about him."

Audrey's mouth wobbled. "Yes."

"What did you say his name was? Finch? That's his surname, I suppose. I haven't heard it as a local name."

"He is from round here, though. He said so. He said he was living right near us for a while – well, he was living near our property, before we came here. He's Bill Brewer's nephew." She flushed. "Oh. I wasn't supposed to say that."

"Why on earth not?"

"Um – it's a bit tricky."

Immediately Mum looked intrigued. "Why?"

"Well, you like Bill Brewer, don't you?"

"He seems a decent person. So yes, I like him. But?"

Audrey fidgeted. Should she say something to Mum about why Finch had run away? She'd promised Finch she wouldn't – another promise she'd said she wouldn't break. But did that really matter now?

She thought of Finch in the candlelit cave, Snowy curled up beside him, the dimness and silence. The gentle piping of the emu-wrens. The astonishing sweep of the dawn sky. She stared down at the floor, concentrating on the pattern in the carpet so she wouldn't cry.

Mum took her hand, and its familiar warmth made Audrey's tears overflow at last. Mum gave her a tissue. "What's the problem?" she asked. "I'll help if I can."

"Maybe I'd better tell Dad too."

Mum looked slightly hurt. "Oh, all right." She raised her voice. "Ian – come here a minute, would you?"

And at last Audrey told them everything: how Finch had worked for Bill Brewer and Bill Brewer hadn't paid him, how he'd beaten the boy and his dog, how in the end Finch had run away and gone to live in the cave.

Dad looked grave. "You're making some pretty major accusations there, Audrey. That's child abuse you're talking about."

"I know."

Mum chimed in. "We've got no evidence. We've never even seen this boy–"

"I have."

"He could be lying–"

"He wouldn't lie."

Dad thought for a while, and then he said, "Audrey, what do you want us to do? If there's any truth in what you say, it's a matter for the police. But first we need to see your friend and talk to him, find out the facts. How bad was the abuse? We don't know. What if your friend was making it all up? We don't know that, either. All we have is what you've told us."

"Finch is totally honest. I know he is. He's just – just–" *He's just so nice.* But Audrey couldn't say it. The tears began to fall again.

Mum passed her another tissue. "I know you'd think that, darling, but people can lie for all sorts of reasons. Maybe this boy was in trouble with the police. Maybe his own family threw him out, for whatever reason. Maybe he's got a drug problem. It might be nothing at all to do with Bill Brewer."

"I have to say," said Dad, "that Bill seems an okay sort of bloke."

Audrey pulled her hand away from Mum's and sat up. "Dad, they're always the worst! You know how on TV reports about murderers the neighbours always say the murderer was really a quiet, nice person, and they can't believe he could ever have killed ten people."

"Well, as I've already said, there's nothing to be done at this point," said Dad, in his "I'm trying to be patient" voice. "Let's wait till we hear if the

185

police have found the boy."

"Till we hear if he's drowned or not, you mean. If he's dead nobody has to do anything, do they?"

Dad's mouth became a straight line. "That's not what I meant. Look, Audrey–"

Audrey turned away from him and sat down on the sofa beside Chloe. She no longer knew what she really thought. Nothing made sense. Unwillingly, she remembered how annoyed Finch had been when she'd suggested that the police might be able to help him. He'd said he didn't want the cops sticking their noses in. Oh God. Maybe he was a thief after all? Maybe it was possible to be bad *and* nice at the same time.

Halfway through dinner, Dad's mobile rang.

Audrey pushed her plate away. She felt as if she was going to be sick.

Chloe put down her half-drunk glass of milk.

Even Mum stopped eating, and laid her knife and fork neatly on each side of her plate. Nobody spoke.

"Yes, I understand," Dad said into the phone. "Good … Good …" There was a long silence. "Are you sure? … I see … Yes … Yes … Excellent. Thanks very much. Sorry we had to bother you with all this … Sure … Yes, of course … Cheers."

"Well?" asked Mum.

"That was Vince from the police rescue lot," said Dad. "A diver has been into the cave, and he found nothing. No body. So that's a good result, isn't it?"

"Thank goodness for that," Mum said. "You can relax now, Audrey. As we thought, your friend has escaped the flood. I think we can assume that he is perfectly okay."

"Yes," said Audrey. She thought she'd be happier to hear that good news. If only she could be absolutely sure that Finch *was* perfectly okay. But something still wasn't quite right, and she didn't know what it was.

CHAPTER 20

By Monday morning it seemed as though the storm had never happened. When Mum drove Audrey and Chloe home from school the road was nearly dry again, and the ford was crossed by the merest trickle. Light, wispy clouds floated in a blue sky.

"The water in the cave will be down now," Audrey said to Chloe, after school on Tuesday. "I'm going there with Dad, to have a look. We thought maybe Finch might have come back." *Please, please let him be there.* "You want to come?"

"Not really."

"Why not?"

"I feel like a Milo." Chloe opened the fridge door. "*Mum*! We're nearly out of milk."

"Did you hear what I said, Chlo?"

"Yeah." Chloe turned to face her, the milk carton in her hand. "I don't want to go to the cave. What if his ghost is there?"

"Of course his ghost won't be there. He didn't die. There's nothing to be scared of."

"But you don't know where he is, do you? You can't be *sure* he's alive. Nobody's seen him. He might've died in the cave and then his body got washed away. Did anyone think of that?"

"You've been watching too many ghost movies, Chlo." Still, Audrey felt a niggle of fear in the pit of her stomach. Could Chloe be right? She tried to sound reassuring, as much for herself as for her sister. "Of course the police would have thought of that. They're professionals. They'd have looked everywhere. And if he did get washed away, they'd have found his ... his body by now, wouldn't they?"

"Don't care." Chloe hunched her shoulders. "I don't want to go. It feels sort of creepy. Just you and Dad go." She stirred Milo into her milk and licked the spoon. With a sticky brown line of Milo on her upper lip, she looked like a sad-faced clown.

Dad was in the orchard salvaging the plums not damaged by the storm, chewed by possums or nibbled at by parrots.

"Dad?" said Audrey. "Can we go to the cave now? I've got my torch."

"Right you are." Dad put both hands on her shoulders and looked her straight in the eyes. "You're not worried about this, are you, Audrey? We're only going to the cave to see if we can find out anything more about this boy, and make double sure everything's okay."

"I'm not worried." *Of course it will be okay. Why wouldn't it be?* But that niggle of fear wouldn't go away.

Dad carried the half-full bucket of plums back to the house and put it on the verandah. "Come along, daughter-of-mine."

Audrey almost reached out to take Dad's hand, something she hadn't done since she was really little. She remembered just in time, before she made herself look babyish. After all, she was almost a teenager.

The grass on the hillside was dry now, although the earth was still damp and soft, and the creek had turned back into a well-behaved stream. Murky water bubbled over the stones and swirled in foamy bays and inlets. Twigs and clots of debris nudged against the banks and were caught in nearby tree branches. The high-water mark showed on the rocks as a stippled line of dirt.

The mouth of the cave was visible again, a darker shadow in the shade of the rocks. Above it the trunk and branches of the crooked tree were a pale scribble against the sky.

A raven cawed. *Corvus coronoides.* Then another, and another. Scavengers. They lifted and circled, and then alighted again. What had they seen?

Audrey walked slowly to the cave, and peered into the entrance. No light, no sign of life. She could feel the blood pulsing in her ears.

"Finch? Are you there?"

Flies buzzed: a whiff of decay.

Panic.

"Dad, it smells like something's dead."

Dad pointed a few metres further down the bank

to a heap of grey fur. "It's just a possum. Must've drowned."

"Oh!" *Only a possum.* Weak with relief, Audrey stuck her head into the cave entrance again. "Finch?" Her voice sounded weak and thready. "It's me."

There was a cold exhalation of air, a reek of dampness and age. The cave seemed secretive, almost sinister. It breathed death.

Could anyone really have lived here? Now, in the bright daylight, with Dad at her side, it seemed to Audrey completely impossible. Finch was certainly not there. But if he had managed to get out safely, perhaps he'd left something behind – a sign? A message? "I'm going in, Dad." She switched on her little penlight torch, squeezed down the narrow passageway and emerged into the main chamber.

Under her feet the sandy floor was wet: it was like walking on the beach after the tide has gone out. When she raised the torch she could see that the cave walls were still shining with moisture. Even so, it was hard to imagine that the chamber had been flooded only a couple of days earlier. The creek must have started to go down almost immediately.

Dad shuffled in after her, so tall that he couldn't

stand up straight even where the cave roof was highest. "Empty," he said. "It doesn't look like there's ever been anyone here."

Taking the torch from Audrey, he shone it around.

The light briefly illuminated the floor and walls, and swung across the ceiling. Audrey could see that the cave chamber had been scoured bare. Not so much as a tin can or a shred of clothing remained.

"There was quite a lot of stuff in here," she told Dad. "Pots and things. Finch must've taken it all. He used this big flat stone as a sort of table."

"Probably anything he didn't take would have been washed away by the flood."

They stood there, silent. *It's a bit like being in a church*, Audrey decided, remembering a visit to the city's cathedral. *The coolness, and the quiet.*

"What's that hollow?" asked Dad, pointing the torch. He peered down the beam of light. "I reckon it could be the start of another cave. I wonder if the police diver saw that one? If the place was full of water they could've missed it."

Another cave? What if he's there? What if he didn't get out? Audrey felt as if her heart had stopped. Then it started to beat again. "When I was here I never saw another cave," she said. "It was always pretty dark, though. I think Finch had a pile of clothes and stuff over there."

Dad walked up to the opening and knelt down. "There's something in here."

"Clothes?" *Please be only clothes.*

"No, it's not clothes." Dad aimed the torch. "It looks like animal bones. They must've been exposed when the water receded. Here, have a look. There's a skull, and a rib cage. It seems pretty complete."

Audrey stared past Dad's shoulder at what the bright circle of light revealed. "What is it? Another possum?"

Dad used his hand to sweep away the wet sand. Now the bones showed up sharp and white. "No, it's bigger than a possum. It could be a fox. It's the right size, and look at that skull. That's a fox's skull, unless I'm much mistaken."

"I think you're right, Dad." Audrey took a deep breath, and let it out slowly. What had she expected?

"The poor old fox probably took shelter on a dark and stormy night and died here."

"I guess so." Audrey reached out to touch the

small skull. Then she looked more closely. What was that around the skeleton's neck? A shred of leather, a rusted buckle. A collar. A dog collar.

A dog.

Snowy?

No, of course not. It can't be. This skeleton's been buried in the cave for years. No way can it be Snowy. It's just a dog. Someone else's dog.

"Dad, it's a dog. Look, there's a collar."

"So there is. I wonder what his story was? Hang on, let's check to make quite sure there's nothing else in here." Dad flashed the torch all the way around the smaller cave, craning his neck to see. After a few seconds he eased himself back. "Completely empty." He got to his feet, bumping his head on the rocky roof. "Ouch! How anyone could bear to live here beats me. Caves spook me at the best of times."

Back outside again, Audrey felt that a huge load had been lifted from her shoulders. Finch was okay! Of course someone like Finch could look after himself. He must've got out before the cave flooded. But where was he now?

CHAPTER 21

Audrey batted away a mosquito, almost slapping Chloe as she did so. They were sitting on the verandah step, under the glory vine. She and Dad hadn't got home till nearly sunset, and the backyard was alive with the chirring of crickets. "There weren't any ghosts, Chlo. But there was a skeleton, a dog—"

In the dusky light Chloe's pale face was almost luminous. "Was it the boy's dog?"

"It couldn't be – it was a skeleton, just bones. Dad thought it was a fox at first. It must've been there for years and years." Audrey thought about that for a moment, and then pushed the thought away. "But everything in the cave was gone, all Finch's things."

"Where d'you think he went? Where would he go?"

"Maybe he hitched a lift to his mum and dad's place. That's what I'd do."

"No, you wouldn't, Aud. You know what Mum says about getting lifts from strangers. You wouldn't be that stupid."

"He could have been desperate, though. People do stupid things when they're desperate." Audrey hated the thought of Finch being desperate, alone, perhaps even scared. "Or maybe … maybe he went with somebody he knows. His family comes from around here. He must know plenty of people."

Chloe was resting her chin in her hand. She rubbed the bridge of her nose with one finger, the way she did when she was thinking hard. After a while she said, "He knows you, too, and he knows where you live. We're closer to the cave than anyone else. Why didn't he come here if he needed help?"

"You're right, Chlo. That doesn't make sense, does it? And I remember telling him we'd help him, so he'd have known he'd be safe with us." *We're friends, Finch and me. Why didn't he come here?*

While Audrey was puzzling over this, Chloe grabbed her arm. "Finch is probably with his parents already. So – why don't we *phone* them?"

"How would we do that? We don't know where they're living, or what Finch's parents' names are. His folks probably aren't on the phone anyway. Hardly anyone has landlines any more."

"Finch's parents would have a mobile," Chloe said. "Maybe *Finch* has a mobile. Just about all kids do. Kids with nice parents," she added, "not mean parents like ours."

"And if he *does* have a mobile, how do we get the number?"

"Oh." Chloe looked downcast. "I'm only trying to help."

"I know." But what Chloe said had set Audrey wondering, again. *Did Finch have a mobile? I should've asked him. I could've given him Dad's number.* As soon as she thought it, she realised how impossible it was. Finch owned hardly anything. No way would he have had a mobile. "Look, I'm sure he's okay. Really."

"I hope so. You need all the friends you can get."

"Thanks."

"You're welcome, Nerd Girl."

Audrey sighed. "Finch was nice," she said, half to herself. "I mean, he *is* nice. You'd like him too, Chlo, I know you would."

Chloe leaned forward, her eyes bright with interest. "Tell me about him, Aud. What's he like? Tall, short, cool, not cool?"

"He's tall and skinny. And kind of cool, I guess. It's hard to say, because actually I never saw him properly. It was dark in the cave, and I never saw him in daylight." (*How weird is that?*) "But he looks kind of … nice. Nerdy and nice."

"So he's *nice*, then, is he, Aud?" Chloe put on her most knowing face. "*Really* nice?"

"Yes." Then Audrey decided to be honest. "His clothes are really, really uncool, though."

"He's perfect for you, then, isn't he?" Chloe said, looking even more knowing. "Nice and nerdy and uncool. Ooh, Aud, are you in *love* with him?"

"Chlo, grow a brain. He's a friend, okay? Just a friend. He's … he's sort of what I imagine a brother would be like. A big brother."

"That's what *you* say. It's not what *I* say."

"As if *you'd* know, you're just a baby."

They went on arguing in a friendly, half-hearted sort of way until Mum called them in for dinner.

The week dragged on. There was no news of Finch. No message from the police, no report in the local newspaper, nothing. Audrey still hadn't quite given up hope that one day he might turn up at their back door, smiling his shy lopsided smile. Perhaps he'd say he was sorry he'd run off on that Sunday morning without saying goodbye. Perhaps he'd explain why he hadn't asked her for help when the floods came. Perhaps he'd apologise for the anxiety he'd caused – not just to her, of course, but to everyone: her parents, the SES people, the police.

She still dreamed that this might happen.

But it didn't.

Every day followed the same boring pattern. School, and home. School, and sports practice, and home. School and home. And at last the weekend again.

"Audrey, I want you to go round to Mavis's place," said Mum. Chloe had been picked up by Emma and her mum and was playing tennis in town; everyone else in the family was having their usual Saturday morning relaxing time.

Audrey, with Freddy curled up beside her, was lying on the sofa reading. She sighed loudly. "Oh, Mum, why? Can't it wait?"

Mum gave her a stern look. "I have a book on preserving fruit that Mavis very kindly lent me, and I should return it. And since I can't use all our plums, I want you to take her a bucketful. They're overripe, and they should be cooked up as soon as possible."

"Why don't you make some jam? You could sell it at the CAW, and be a real country person."

"It's the CWA, Audrey. And I don't want to argue about this. You don't have to stay long. Just drop the things off and come straight home."

Audrey rolled off the sofa and landed on the floor, taking Freddy with her. Freddy walked away with his ears back, looking deeply offended.

"Now you've upset Fred," Audrey said. "This visit to Mavis had better be worth it."

"This is an unexpected pleasure," said Mavis. "Come in, Audrey. Thanks for the plums. That's real kind of your mum. Now, if you'll hang on a bit, I've got some magazines she might like to read."

Audrey followed her down the hallway, stopping for a moment to look at the painting of the emu-wrens. The detail was fantastic, and the artist had even captured something of the spirit of the little birds. Her mind went back to that morning with Finch, and the thrill she'd felt when she saw the tiny emu-wrens flitting about among the ferns.

"Take a seat," said Mavis over her shoulder. "I'll find the mags, and then I'll get you some morning tea."

"Thanks." Audrey went into the kitchen and sat down. The room was very quiet apart from the ticking of the clock on the mantelpiece.

After a little while Mavis came back. She plonked a pile of cookery magazines on the table (*Wow! Mum'll be thrilled*), and then put the round flowered tin next to it. Taking the lid off with a flourish, she revealed a fat chocolate cake smothered in icing. "I made a couple for the CWA trading table, and this one sank in the middle. Looks a bit like a bomb crater, doesn't it?" She cut a big slice for Audrey and a smaller one for herself, and then poured two glasses of lemon cordial.

"So how're things at your place?"

"Pretty good."

"Mum and Dad okay?"

"Yes, thanks."

"And what've you been up to?" Her blue eyes gazed kindly at Audrey.

"Nothing much." Audrey swallowed a mouthful of chocolate cake. It was even better than the Anzacs. "Oh, there is something." *I might as well tell her now – what does it matter?* "You'll never guess, a while ago I saw some southern emu-wrens. Two males and a female."

Mavis sat forward, beaming. "Well, isn't that a bit of news! Where did you find them?"

Audrey smiled too. It was good to be able to share this with Mavis at last. "You probably know the place. It's that bit of swamp near the waterhole on Frank Blix's land. I was there with, um, a friend. He said there's always emu-wrens there."

"Hang on," said Mavis. "That's not Frank Blix's land. It belongs to my brother, or it did. Frank Blix, funny old chap that he was, he died way back in the nineteen-forties. My brother bought the property from Frank's son ... let me think ... nearly thirty years ago."

"Oh." Audrey was confused. "My friend might've only called it Frank Blix's land because that's what it was known as, but – no, he meant it, because he said Frank Blix was really old. I remember he said that."

"Not to worry," said Mavis. "Whatever you want to call it, that land is mine now. My brother, dear soul, he left it to me in his will. He always loved the bush – I guess you'd call him a greenie nowadays. He wanted the land to be kept like a nature reserve, a bit of natural bushland among all these vineyards that are taking over the country. He always reckoned there were emu-wrens there, but I never saw any. They're such shy little fellas. You'll have to show me where you found them." She patted Audrey's arm. "You know you can explore there whenever you like. I'd be real happy to have someone enjoy it, particularly a bird-lover like yourself."

"Thanks, that'd be great." Audrey looked down at the table.

Mavis nodded. "You would've got on well with

my brother. He loved his birds. Knew a lot about 'em, too.'

Something isn't right here, Audrey thought. *Why would Finch have said Frank Blix was alive when he wasn't?* "Old Frank Blix is ninety not out" – that was what he'd said, wasn't it?

"Your brother–" she started. She stopped, and then tried again. "Did your brother live on that bit of land, you know, where the emu-wrens are?"

"Yeah, that's where he went after he retired. He built a cabin on the far boundary, where there's a nice view of the sea, and he spent most of his time there drawing birds. You know that painting of emu-wrens in the hall? That's his. Birds were always his hobby. He loved aeroplanes too. He went back to school when he was eighteen to get his matric, Year Twelve I suppose you'd call it now, and when he was nineteen he joined the air force and trained as a pilot. He said flying was the biggest thrill you could imagine. Us kids, his brother and sisters, we were that proud of him. He flew Caribou transport planes in the Vietnam War and after he came back home he was a carpenter. He always liked working with wood. Hang on."

She got up and went into the front room, returning with something which she put down in front of Audrey. It was a bird carved from wood. A fat little bird with a short tail. "Know what that is?"

Audrey felt her skin prickle, from her toes right up to her scalp. She nodded. "It's a finch, isn't it." A statement, not a question.

"My brother made it. He gave it to me for my seventh birthday. It's walnut, the wood. Look at the way he's carved the feathers – beautiful, isn't it?"

"You mean your brother who died?"

Mavis's face softened. "Yeah. My big brother, Ross. We buried him two weeks ago last Friday. And that reminds me, I must thank your mum for her card. Very nice of her."

Audrey picked up the little bird. It felt smooth and solid in her hand. *It's the bird Finch showed me. I'm positive it is. But how did she get it?* "Sorry, Mrs – I mean Mavis – what was your brother's name again?"

"Ross. Ross Finch. I was Mavis Finch before I married."

"Your brother is Ross Finch?" Audrey began to tremble now. Her throat contracted until she could scarcely breathe. *Don't be stupid*, she told herself.

It's just a coincidence. Finch is probably the old guy's grandson, and he has the same name. Lots of people are named after their grandparents.

"That's right. He kept to himself after his wife died, but people around here had a lot of respect for him and what he stood for. Conservation and that – caring for the land and its creatures. He was a very sick man this last year. I miss him, but I wasn't sorry to see him go, if you know what I mean. His time had come." She looked at Audrey closely. "Are you all right? You going to throw up?"

"No, I'm fine." Audrey struggled to focus. "He told me there was Pete and Lizzy and May," she said. "The youngest girl was called May. He didn't have a sister called Mavis."

Mavis stared at her. "How on God's green earth do you know about my family? You never got to meet Ross, did you?"

"There was no Mavis."

"The family always called me May." Mavis gave her a puzzled look. "Does that help? Though, mind you, I don't have the faintest idea what's going on here."

Suddenly Audrey thought of Finch's uncle, Bill

Brewer. But now, who was Bill Brewer?

She gulped her cordial. Its cold sweetness was reassuring. "Mavis, are you really Bill Brewer's aunty?"

This was safer ground.

"Bill's granddad was my uncle," Mavis said, "my mum's brother. We never saw much of him once we moved away from the district, but Ross stayed up here and worked for him for a while. It would've been around 1947 – it was after the war, although people were still getting over it. But," she added thoughtfully, "there was something strange about that time Ross was with Uncle Bill."

Audrey drank some more cordial. "Was there?"

Mavis settled back in her chair. "We never heard much about it. Ross never complained about a thing – he was as tough as you like, and proud. But there was a time back there when he vanished for a few weeks. We didn't know about it till years later. My dad reckoned Ross might've run away – Uncle Bill was tight with his money and he could be a bit of a … well, let's say we found out he had a dark side. Anyhow, it turns out that Ross disappeared, and after a while Uncle Bill got on to the police. He said someone'd been thieving from his property, and he reckoned it was Ross. Only small stuff, you know, food and that. Ross was never a crook.

"Our mum was worried sick, with the police coming round, and nobody knowing where Ross was. But then one day he turned up at our house. He'd got himself a job working for the post office, delivering telegrams. I don't suppose you know what they are, do you? We could see he'd been through a bad time – he was skin and bone – but he never talked about it, ever. I remember his little dog had died, and he was that cut up about it. He loved that dog." She frowned. "What was his name, now? The little dog's name?"

"Snowy," said Audrey.

"Snowy. That's the one." Mavis looked at her, and her eyes were Finch's eyes, blue and alive in her creased old face.

Audrey breathed out, and then in again. Her heart thudded. "That's who the little fox terrier was, the one we thought might be a stray. He was living with your brother in the cave on Frank Blix's property. I know it doesn't make sense, but that little dog was Snowy. He was your brother's dog."

"Ross's dog? No, no, that's not possible. It couldn't be."

"I promise you, Ross was there. He was living in the cave, and so was Snowy. I can't explain it. That's how I know him. That's how I know about all of you." Audrey took another deep breath. "He said his name was Ross, but everyone called him Finch."

The clock ticked.

"I saw him carving that wooden bird for you," Audrey said softly. "He wanted to give it to you for your birthday. Your seventh birthday."

"Imagine that." Mavis's eyes were filled with wonder. "Well, time's a funny thing, and I don't pretend to understand it. But would you believe me if I told you that right now I'm only seven years old?"

"Yes," said Audrey. "Yes, I would."

CHAPTER 22

"It makes my head hurt," said Chloe. She and Audrey were sitting cross-legged on the clover lawn under the clothes line. It was a warm, sunny day. In their cage nearby the finches were cheeping contentedly.

"I know."

"Who'd believe it?"

"I'm not even sure *I* believe it." Audrey was silent, thinking, although she'd already been over it all, in her mind, a thousand times.

"Audrey–" Chloe turned to face her, "–when Finch died a couple of weeks ago, he was *eighty-five*."

Audrey nodded.

"So when you saw him he was a *ghost*."

"No, he wasn't. He was never a ghost, because he was still alive. He was *there*. Don't you see?" How slippery the facts were, how hard to make sense of! "But then he died, I mean, he *really* died, you know, in real time, and after that he wasn't there any more. When the cave flooded, he'd already gone."

Chloe sighed. "I still don't understand."

"I can't explain it any better. I wish I could. And there's another thing. When I saw Finch that last time, when he showed me the emu-wrens, he told me to come round to the cave again. He promised me he'd be there. He said, 'I'll be there, I promise.' I keep wondering why he said that. I mean, he must have *known*."

"Known what?"

"That he had no more time left."

There was a long silence, and then Chloe said, "So he was alive, and he wasn't a ghost. Was he, like, real? I mean, could you touch him?"

Audrey considered this. "I don't know. I mean, I never got really close to him. We just talked lots. But he *seemed* so real. Maybe I just wanted him to be real."

"What about his dog?"

"Snowy never wanted me to pat him or anything. He always moved away. I just thought he probably wouldn't go to anybody but Finch. It sort of makes sense now." She paused, thinking. "Chlo, I just realised something. Nobody ever saw Finch or Snowy except me."

"And Freddy, don't forget. Freddy saw the dog first."

"You're right – Fred saw him too. I wonder why? D'you think it's because animals know stuff that people don't? Like they have extrasensory perception?"

"Extra *what*?"

"Animals are supposed to see things we can't see. They *sense* them somehow."

"That's so weird," Chloe said. Then she giggled. "Does that mean you're an animal, Aud?"

"Of course I'm an animal. So are you. We're all animals." *He told me I was brainy. He said, "I'm glad I know you."*

They sat there, listening to the finches. Then Chloe said, "So it *was* Finch's dog, the skeleton you found. Are you going to leave him in the cave?"

"I think so. That's where he belongs. I'll go down there and bury him properly."

"What d'you think happened to him?"

"Maybe he was bitten by a snake. Maybe he ate poison meant for foxes." Audrey shuddered. "Finch must've buried him there. I bet that was the reason he left the cave. He told me he didn't think he'd be able to stay there if anything happened to Snowy. It could've been one of the reasons he came back to the cave, too. Because Snowy was still there."

Chloe got to her feet. "Poor little dog. Poor Finch." Her face brightened. "Hey, you said that land belongs to Mavis now? That means we can go there whenever we want! You can show me where the emu-finches are!"

"You mean the emu-*wrens*. Why would you want to see them? You're not interested in birds."

"I might be. Ms Petersen wants us to do a conservation project, and I'm doing mine on things that are endangered. Emu-wrens are endangered, aren't they?" She looked down at Audrey. "You want to help me?"

They stood beside the waterhole, Audrey, Chloe and Mavis, shivering in the cold air of early dawn. The countryside was waking up. The strident call of a wattlebird could be heard from a distant tree and, much further away, the faint crowing of a rooster.

Audrey had brought her camera, last year's Christmas present, to photograph the emu-wrens. She'd already practised photographing the wattlebirds and taken a few shots of the waterhole and the stretch of swampland. Then she'd snapped a dozy rabbit that had come to within a few metres of them.

"Look, a bunny!" Chloe screamed as the rabbit hopped away in alarm, its white tail bobbing. "Oh, it's so cute!"

"You wouldn't say that if you'd seen a rabbit plague," Mavis said drily. "Rabbits destroy the countryside like nothing else – eat everything in sight. An environmental nightmare, that's your bunny."

"They're still cute, though," said Chloe.

Audrey decided to change the subject. "Look,"

she said, turning the camera around and showing the photograph to Mavis.

Mavis stared at the tiny camera screen in amazement. "That's not bad, is it? I don't understand how these things work, mind you. Seems like some kind of magic. But then I still don't understand television – all those pictures zooming through the air."

Chloe jumped up and down, flapping her arms to keep warm. "Where are the emu-wrens, Audrey? You said they'd be here."

"They *were* here. They *are* here. Be patient. And stop jumping around, you'll scare them away."

Chloe stopped jumping and started chewing a fingernail. Then she pulled her finger out of her mouth and pointed. "There!"

Mavis and Audrey swung around. "Where?"

"Sorry. It was another bunny."

Audrey groaned. "Chlo, birds don't have ears."

They were all silent again.

They waited, and waited.

Nothing.

"Well," Mavis said at last, "I've nearly frozen my bottom off, so I reckon we should call it a day. I suppose the little fellas just weren't ready to come out and say hello. How about I show you my brother's house instead? It's not far from here. I'd like you to see it, if you're interested."

"We're interested," said Audrey. "Aren't we, Chlo?"

Chloe made a face. "I guess so."

"Follow me," said Mavis.

A track wound through low scrub and she-oaks and led them up a rise into a grove of trees and shrubs – lemon-scented gums, wattles, bottlebrushes. Hidden parrots squawked and whistled: there was the sweet *ting! ting!* of an eastern rosella.

"Ross planted things that would attract the birds," Mavis said.

Behind a dense hedge of banksias was a small timber house. It had the lonely, rather downtrodden look of a place where nobody was living. Grey drifts of spider web were caught in the window frames, and creepers wound up the verandah posts.

Mavis unlocked the front door.

"It's a good little hide-out," she said. "In fact, I've decided I'll sell my old place and move in. All it needs is a good dust and a bit of a clean-up, and it'll suit me and Daphne just fine. I think Ross'd be happy with that."

There wasn't much furniture inside the hut. A bed. A table. A workbench. Above the bench was a shelf crowded with branches, dried flowers, wood carvings, rock specimens and what looked like a few fossils. The bench itself was covered with sketchbooks and art paper, coloured pencils and paintbrushes thrust into jars, geometrical equipment, masking tape, a scalpel. There were dozens of photographs of birds, and a scattering of bird feathers, from downy breast feathers to sturdy pinions. A stuffed magpie sat on a perch, its head permanently cocked as its brown glass eye searched for non-existent grubs.

Audrey picked up a sketchbook and turned the pages with careful fingers. Pencil sketches of bird feet, beaks, lightning impressions of parrots in flight, details of feathers–

She turned to Mavis. "He was *good*, wasn't he? Awesome. Where did he learn to draw?"

"Self-taught, believe it or not. He really got into it after he retired. Never showed his work or anything like that. Just did it for himself." She opened a long drawer under the workbench and took out a pile of watercolour paintings on thick art paper. Dozens of them, nearly all of birds. Audrey gasped. Magpies. Blue wrens. Diamond-tailed finches. Black ducks. A pair of peregrine falcons. A clutch of honeyeaters, and a willie wagtail on a fence post. A boobook owl. A white-faced heron. And a sketched impression of an emu-wren – only one this time – a male. A bright eye, a puff of feathers. And that extraordinary tail.

Chloe craned her neck to see. "That's an emu-wren, isn't it? It's so cute! I wish we'd seen some this morning. That would've been *so* excellent." She humphed. "I don't know what to do my project on now."

"It was bad luck we didn't see them." But at the exact moment she said this, Audrey had an idea. "I know what you can do instead, though."

"What?"

"Finch."

"*What?*" Chloe scowled. "Why would I want to do a project on your *finches?*"

"Not *my* finches. *Finch.* It's perfect! He's an important local person. Or he was," she corrected herself. "And he helped with conservation, like buying this land so it wouldn't be developed. And he was a brilliant artist. I could help you, if you like. We could take some photos of things around here – this bench, and the house, and stuff. What d'you think?"

"Yeah! Great idea!" Chloe bounced with delight.

Mavis carefully laid the paintings out on the bench. "Audrey, I'd like you to have something in memory of Ross. You too," she added, seeing Chloe's lower lip begin to droop. "You can choose a painting as well."

"Oh!" Chloe said. She moved her hand over the bench, darting it back and forth and finally picking up the watercolour of the willie wagtail. "Can I have this?"

"Of course you can. And Audrey, what would you like?"

"They're all really beautiful. But I'd like the emu-wren." Tears came into her eyes, and she blinked hard to keep them from falling. "It has to be the emu-wren, doesn't it?"

Mavis smiled at her, and it was Finch's smile. "I reckon so," she said.

CHAPTER 23

The scrub glowed golden, bathed in sunshine. Audrey had just seen the three emu-wrens again, and amazingly, impossibly, one of them had flitted right up to her and perched on her finger. It looked at her, its tiny dark eyes sparkling – she almost expected it to speak. It was a moment of pure happiness. Then an odd noise edged its way into her head. A harsh sort of wailing noise. Could it be a wattlebird? No, it wasn't a wattlebird. What was it?

Slowly Audrey opened her eyes. As the vision of the emu-wrens faded, she felt a deep disappointment. Of course – it had been a dream. Reality told her that the wailing sound was Freddy, calling her. She rolled over, slid out of bed and stumbled down the hallway.

In the darkness of the kitchen the screen back door was a rectangle of pale grey. Freddy was nuzzling it, rubbing his back along it, making little purring noises in his throat.

"Okay, Fred." Audrey looked at the digital clock on the microwave: nearly five-thirty. "I guess it's late enough. Out you go." *I'm sick of this. I must train Fred to use a litter tray.*

She opened the door, watched as Freddy bounded away over the lawn, and then closed it. Yawning, she made her way back to bed and crawled under the quilt.

Sleep.

She decided not to go back to the waterhole after school. She'd been planning to – she wanted to have another go at finding the emu-wrens – but it was getting late, so instead she went to the cave. She didn't tell anybody where she was going. This was something she had to do by herself.

She took the torch with her, and a garden trowel. It was big enough for all the digging she'd have to do.

When she reached the cave entrance, she hesitated, unsure. For a moment she felt almost afraid. But the place now seemed neither welcoming nor sinister.

It's just rocks, she told herself. *It's just a cave.*

Inside the main chamber there was absolute blackness, absolute silence except for the sound of her own breathing. The dark reached out to her, velvet-soft. She stood there, eyes closed, remembering Finch. This had been his home, and he'd been free and happy here. Alone, but not lonely. Was that why he'd come back, to re-live this time in his life? And then he'd lost the little dog he loved so much, and the loneliness became too much to bear.

After a while, bit by bit, Audrey felt the cave begin to come alive. The air moved gently, and darker shadows appeared in the darkness. A whisper of warmth grew warmer, surrounding her, embracing her. She felt safe, protected, completely unafraid.

I'm not alone, she thought. *Finch promised me he'd*

be here in the cave, and he's here now, I know it. Others, too. Lots of others. I can feel them all around me.

She didn't know how long she stood there before the spell was broken and she was aware of coldness and damp. She switched on her torch, and in its glare the shadows retreated and vanished. The cave was just a cave again.

Audrey sighed, and shivered.

Inside the smaller chamber Snowy's skeleton still lay partly uncovered. She crouched beside it and gazed at it for a long time. Lightly, barely touching them, she stroked the eroded bones.

"Good boy," she whispered. "Good dog."

As soon as she'd said the words, a huge lump came into her throat. She cried as Finch must have cried, gutted with loss, and the raw animal sound echoed all around her.

She cried until she could cry no more. Then, very tenderly, as if folding a blanket over them, she began to cover the bones.

CHAPTER 24

"*Please* don't feed sweet things to the cat," Mum said. "They're so bad for him. He's a carnivore. He should only eat meat."

"But it's the Easter holidays," said Audrey. "I know he's not allowed to have chocolate, but can't he have a little bit of hot cross bun?" She scratched Freddy's head. "You like hot cross bun, don't you, Fred?"

Freddy daintily licked up the offered buttery scrap.

"See? He loves it."

Mum shook her head as she pushed open the

back door and walked outside with a basket of wet washing. "He'll get fat," she said over her shoulder.

"*I'll* get fat," said Chloe, slumping over the kitchen table. "I'm so full of chocolate I can't *move*." She sat up again. "Aud, did I tell you Emma's mum's taking me and Emma to the city on Wednesday? We're going shopping, and then we'll go to that ice cream place in the mall. Bubblegum gelato, yay!"

"Sounds great," said Audrey. She helped herself to one of her mini Easter eggs, peeled off the foil and folded it neatly into a thin strip. Her mouth full of chocolate, she walked over to the kitchen window and looked out. The rows of vines were golden now. High on the hill, beyond the orchard, a bright red tractor was slowly turning the far paddock into brown corduroy.

Life in the country was turning out to be all right. Actually, it was even better than all right. It had taken a little while, but now Audrey felt that she was finally at home. The farm was a place where she fitted, exactly. It was solid and comfortable and real.

School was good, too. She was near the top of the class in most subjects, and right at the top in maths and science. So far she didn't have a best friend, but she didn't feel lonely. She was part of a group. And there was always the chance that her sort-of friends might one day be real friends.

One of the best things about school was Mr Scardino. He was really kind, really easy to talk to, a bit like Finch had been. He was going to organise extra art lessons for her in third term, which would be brilliant. When she'd told Mavis, Mavis had given her all Finch's art materials – lots of excellent stuff. She'd said she was only too pleased to find a good home for it.

Using Finch's brushes and pencils made Audrey feel sort of sad and sort of happy at the same time. Sometimes, when she was drawing, she felt that he was standing next to her, his hands guiding hers, correcting and refining her line work. If she turned her head very quickly, she imagined she might just catch a glimpse of him.

She hadn't told Mr Scardino about Finch. Well, that wasn't quite true. She'd told him how the conservationist Ross Finch had also been this amazingly talented artist nobody knew about, but she hadn't told him about the person she thought of as the real Finch, the boy who'd been her friend.

Not yet, anyhow. Maybe one day.

Dad was working hard on his new vineyard. He was putting in five more hectares of vines, grenache and pinot noir this time. And Mum had started a part-time job at Goosey Gander, helping Emma's mum and doing the bookkeeping.

Audrey turned to Chloe. "Did you know Mavis has moved into Finch's old place? She's sold her house already."

"I heard Mum and Dad talking about it. Maybe we'll get a new family living down the road."

"Maybe." Audrey considered this. It could be good – depending on what the family was like. Maybe there'd be a boy like Finch. But no, nobody else could be like Finch.

She peeled another chocolate egg and popped it into her mouth. *Last one.* "I'm going birdwatching with Mavis next weekend."

She waited, but there was no response.

"Chlo?"

Chloe was flicking through the fashion pages of a department store catalogue. Dad had given her twenty dollars as a reward when she got top marks for her conservation project, and she'd told Audrey she was going to spend it when she went shopping with Emma.

"What did you say, Aud?"

"I'm going birdwatching with Mavis. Well, not just Mavis. There's about six of us, and we're going up to the ranges. There could be some flame robins up there, and Mavis said she's almost positive she saw a brown treecreeper a couple of weeks ago. It's hard to see them because they have such good camouflage. Chel likes bushwalking, so she's coming too. You want to come with us?"

Chloe shook her head vigorously. "I don't think so."

"Mavis says there are at least a hundred different species around here. I've started to make a list of all the ones I've seen, and so far I've got more than thirty. Actually, thirty-three—"

"Maybe only thirty-two," Chloe said.

"What? I'm talking about *species*. That's different *kinds* of birds, not numbers."

"Freddy ate one of the species, then. Sorry, I meant to tell you. I saw some feathers at the back of the tank-stand, I think it was Friday. I don't know what sort of feathers they were. There were bits of black and white."

"It mightn't have been Freddy." But Audrey felt a sharp twinge of fear. *Oh, Fred.*

"I was hoping like crazy it wasn't. I mean, Fred doesn't do things like that, does he? I thought it might be another cat. Then I saw him after, and he still had a bit of fluff stuck to his mouth, so ..."

"Show me," Audrey said.

There wasn't much to see, after all, just a small pile of downy breast-feathers and a few pinions. They stared at it in silence.

"I still love him," Chloe said, almost tearfully. "I know he's been naughty, but I still love him."

"I know, Chlo. So do I."

"He's still our kitty."

"Of course he is."

"He'll probably never do it again."

"We just have to make sure he doesn't. Oh God, I let him out this morning, didn't I? I should stop doing that. It was just before five o'clock, way too early. Perhaps ..." But she didn't want to think any more about *perhaps.*

"What sort of bird do you think it was?" Chloe asked, poking at the feathers with her foot.

"I'm not sure," Audrey said. "There's not much of it left, but I think it was most likely a New Holland honeyeater. *Phylidonyris novaehollandiae*. See, there's a bit of yellow? That's from a wing."

Chloe stooped to pick up one of the bright feathers. "Why would Fred do it? It's not like we don't feed him."

"He's a cat, Chlo. It's like Mavis says, they don't change. Once a cat, always a cat. They hunt things. It's in their nature." She stopped. "Why are you looking at me like that?"

"You talk about Mavis a lot."

"Do I?" Audrey thought about that as they walked slowly back towards the house. It was a relief to concentrate on something apart from Freddy and the terrible thing he'd done. "I think it's because I really like her," she said at last. "We're friends. I know she's old but it doesn't make any difference, it's just part of who she is. And she reminds me of Finch. Does that make sense?"

"I guess so."

"And she knows heaps. She's kind of like a wise old owl. *Tyto alba*." Audrey looked sideways at Chloe. "That's a barn owl to you."

Chloe aimed a pretend smack at her. "You'll never change either, Aud. Once a nerd, always a nerd. *Nerdo audrey*." She stuck the yellow feather in her hair. "If Mavis is an owl, what am I?"

"You're a rainbow lorikeet. *Trichoglossus moluccanus*. Noisy and greedy and very cheeky."

"That's a horrible name."

"Can't help it. Lorikeets are heaps pretty, though."

"Okay, I'll be a lorikeet. So what bird are you, Aud?"

"What do you think I am?"

"I was going to say you were some kind of owl, but you can't be if Mavis is an owl too." Chloe stopped walking and rubbed her nose thoughtfully. "You don't like people noticing you, so you have to be a treecreeper or something. Sorry, a *brown* treecreeper."

Audrey shook her head. "I'm not a brown treecreeper. I'm not a brown *anything*. Not any more."

"I give up, then. Tell me."

Audrey closed her eyes and imagined herself hovering, hovering, the whole world spread out beneath her, and then diving—

"I'm a falcon," she said. "A peregrine falcon."

"But falcons are scary, aren't they?" protested Chloe. "They kill things. How can you be a falcon?"

Audrey could still hear Finch's voice in her head. *There's something extra special about falcons.* Aloud, she said, "Because falcons are right at the top of the pecking order, and they know it."

Chloe looked at her curiously. "Are you at the top of the pecking order now?"

"Of course," Audrey said. She hugged her little sister. "That's *exactly* where I am."

EPILOGUE

Freddy loved the early morning. Head up, tail up, whiskers bristling with anticipation, he bounded down the hill towards the creek. The dampness of the grass, the earthy smells of still unfamiliar living things made him feel alert and excited. He investigated tufts of fur and wisps of feather, ancient droppings left by long-gone sheep, tracks of slugs and snails, crickets and woodlice. Occasionally he breathed in the warm, rank aromas left by larger, more recent overnight visitors – passing rabbits and foxes. The excitement of the hunt coursed through his blood, made his eyes grow huge and his pupils dilate.

The creek was his favourite place. Sometimes he caught a frog there, or a shiny little lizard unable to hide in time, his teeth crunching the tiny bones.

He leaped nimbly over the rocks, reaching the far bank in a couple of seconds, impatiently shaking a wet paw.

Along the line of the creek he trotted. In the light of the rising sun the shadow of his small body cast a wavering spidery shadow.

He stopped to drink at the waterhole, his pink tongue lap-lapping. The scrubby land around here was full of interesting surprises. Beetles, mice, baby rabbits, birds. What would he find today? He sniffed a familiar scent beneath a tea-tree. Another cat had been here – an interloper. The musky scent was offensive, unmistakable. His tail bristled slightly.

A faint peeping and rustling caught his attention.

He crouched.

At the fringe of a mass of greenery he saw three small birds. Their jerky, erratic movements were unbearably stimulating. Freddy focused his whole mind on them, pinpointed every fraction of his energy and concentration on those movements. He could smell the little birds' soft feathers, could almost taste the warm blood in their bodies. His jaw began to tremble uncontrollably. The end of his tail twitched.

He waited patiently, a white-and-tabby shadow of a cat, invisible in the mottled shadow of the bush.

The three little birds hopped closer, flirting their long tails. Now one of them separated from the others.

His belly almost touching the ground, Freddy moved slowly, silently towards it.

The two male birds fluttered upwards, sounding the alarm – *See! See! See!* – but the female, slower, stayed on the ground.

Freddy pounced.

ABOUT THE AUTHOR

PENNY MATTHEWS has written more than thirty books for children and young adults. She writes in a variety of genres and has won many awards, including the Children's Book Council of Australia Book of the Year Award (Early Childhood category), the Environment Award for Children's Literature and the Davitt Award for Children's and Young Adult Literature. She lives in Adelaide.